ALIEN MATE
Alien Mate 1

Cara Bristol

Alien Mate
Copyright © April 2017 by Cara Bristol

ISBN: 978-0-9968390-8-2

Editor: Kate Richards
Copy Editor: Nanette Sipe
Proofreader: Meredith Gurr
Cover Artist: Sweet 'N Spicy Designs
Formatting by Wizards in Publishing

Published in the United States of America
Cara Bristol
https://carabristol.com

Chapter One

Starr

Truth would prevail. It *had* to. It had to. It had to.

The space over the empty juror box shimmered, and then a real-time hologram of the jurors materialized. I kept my face expressionless as advised by counsel and clenched my hands in my lap. The jurors avoided my eyes, and hope drained out, leaving me sick inside. My attorney, Maridelle, covered my hand and squeezed.

"Have you reached a verdict?" the judge asked.

"We have, your honor," the foreman replied.

"What say you?"

"We, the members of the jury, find the defendant, Starr Elizabeth Conner, guilty of second-degree murder."

My heart seized in my chest. I wasn't aware of leaping to my feet, but Maridelle caught my arm. "I didn't do it! I'm innocent," I cried. My gaze shot to the prosecution table where People's Attorney Gil Aaronson, a crony of the Carmichael family—although

I couldn't prove it—stowed his CompuBrief in its case. He didn't look at me, either, but a smug smile rested on his face.

Electrocuffs in hand, a bailiff headed toward me.

"We'll appeal, don't worry. We'll get the verdict overturned," Maridelle whispered in my ear as the bailiff fastened the restraints. She'd believed me, but no one else had—how could that bode well for the future? If she hadn't been able to convince my peers of my innocence the first time around, what chance would she have on appeal? The Carmichaels controlled too much. They didn't hold political office themselves. They owned the people who did.

"Sentencing is set for one week." The judge cracked his gavel, and his holographic image wavered and then vaporized. A very solid bailiff hustled me to my cell.

* * * *

A statuesque woman plopped down next to me in the lounge. Her skin reminded me of rich, creamy milk chocolate, the kind only the wealthy could afford. Everyone else bought the synth stuff and pretended it was good. "I'm Andrea Simmons," she said. "Cyber hacking." We introduced ourselves on the *SS Australia* by name and crime.

"Starr Conner...second-degree murder." Maridelle had cautioned not to discuss my case pending the appeal. Big ships have big ears and all that. So, I'd tried to avoid my fellow passengers, keeping to my cabin, venturing to the mess hall when it would be deserted. Eventually, loneliness—or maybe acceptance of my fate—nudged me out of isolation. My conviction had less chance of reversal than I'd had for acquittal the first time around. My presence on the ship demonstrated how well the trial had gone.

Just in case the appeal was successful, I shifted the conversation back to Andrea. "You were convicted of hacking?"

"Yes. Cyber robbery, actually. I was the best in the New Americas!" Her boast confirmed her guilt. She sighed. "I hear Dakon is quite primitive. No computer technology to speak of."

"How did you get caught?"

"Greed. I returned to a site I'd previously hacked, and they'd installed a viral tracker. Busted!" Her eyes narrowed. "Who'd you kill?"

"Nobody. I'm innocent." I'd continue to state that until the end of my days.

She barked out a husky laugh. "We all are. Haven't you heard? There are no guilty people on the *SS*

Australia."

"She killed Jaxon Carmichael." A brunette with a head of bouncy curls piped up with the identity of the "victim" I'd been convicted of bludgeoning to death.

Andrea whistled and eyed me with new respect. "Honey, you roll with the big boys, don't you?"

The brunette shook her head. "How could you not recognize her from the pay-for-view gov-vids of her trial on the 'net? She's a celebrity."

Andrea sniffed. "As a general rule, I avoid the government sites."

"Too risky?" I asked.

"No money there. Terra One World is damn near bankrupt. Why do you think we're on this ship? First, they *save* money by not having to house us in prison, and second, they *make* money from the *illuvian* minerals the Dakonians are paying for us. It's a double dip."

"They sold us into slavery." I stared at my hands. Carmichael "justice" had been swift. While others languished in prison for years awaiting a court date, I'd been tried, convicted, and sentenced in a mere two months. Rocket fast—a contrast to the appeals process which would be evolutionary slow. Sitting in prison waiting for an uncertain outcome didn't appeal, but was *this* better?

"More like presented us with an offer we couldn't refuse." Andrea shrugged.

"What do you mean?"

"We could have finished our sentences. Instead we opted for immediate freedom via one-way shuttle to Dakon."

"You had a choice?" I glanced between Andrea and the other woman.

"The application form spelled it out." The brunette nodded. "The selection process was very competitive. Ninety percent of the women who applied didn't get accepted."

"Application form? I didn't fill out any application form."

Andrea's gaze narrowed. "You didn't complete a profile? Health history, activity levels, physical description..."

"No." I pressed my lips together. Carmichael justice again, which was to say, no justice. They were sending me as far away as they could get me.

"That's odd." Andrea squinted.

Maybe becoming an alien's *companion* wasn't such a terrible fate. We could be friends with very limited benefits. Billions of miles between me and the

Carmichaels couldn't hurt, and it beat spending my life in prison. If the Carmichaels could have me wrongfully convicted, they could block my appeal.

But how would I keep track of the status? Since the planet wasn't connected to the 'net, how would Maridelle update me?

"Well, we're all here now. It's kind of like being a 'net-order bride," the brunette said cheerfully. "By the way, I'm Tessa Chartreuse. I ran an escort service for an elite clientele."

"So why are you here? Prostitution isn't illegal." It had been decriminalized a long time ago.

"No, but money laundering is." She shrugged.

Andrea laughed. "She's an entrepreneur."

I took a deep breath. "Any idea what the aliens look like?" I'd kept to myself, but I'd heard rumors our intended "mates" were scaly blue with long tails. Only recently had Terra One World made contact with Dakon. I'd been told the aliens "looked like us," but I had little confidence in my government to tell the truth.

"I did a little 'net research before they transported me to the shuttle," Andrea explained. "They are humanoid, genetically compatible with us, but they're taller, much more muscular, and bigger." She held her hands about a meter apart.

"Are you talking about their penises or their bodies in general?" Tessa asked.

Shit, I hoped Andrea was referring to their bodies. I eyed the span between her palms.

Andrea rolled her eyes. "Their bodies in general. I did not research their junk."

"It would be proportionate, though, wouldn't you think?" Tessa persisted. You could take the girl out of the escort business, but you couldn't take the escort business out of the girl.

Andrea placed her index fingers to her forehead so they stuck up. "And they have—"

"Antennas?" My jaw dropped.

"More like horns."

"That's worse!"

"Vestigial horns. Mostly hidden by their hair."

"So we're the court-ordered brides of horned aliens who may or may not have big dicks," I said.

"That's the size of it." Andrea snickered.

I got up and moved to the observation window. Without the filtering effects of a planetary atmosphere, stars in space didn't twinkle. They appeared as solid points of light. We'd traveled far enough that none of the constellations were familiar anymore.

"Dakon must be very far away." We'd been on the ship for two months with thirty days left to go.

"It's hyper speed compared to the three-year round trip the first contact took. Thanks to the illuvian ore, we'll do it in three months," Andrea said. "The Dakonians have been waiting a long time for their mates. After the first contact ship returned to Earth, it took a year to set up the program and recruit the first group of women."

Tessa giggled. "They're going to be really horny by now. In more ways than one."

"What happens if they don't like the brides they receive?" I asked Andrea. She seemed to be in the know.

"Then we'll be sent back to serve out the remainder of our sentence," she replied. "With credit for time served on Dakon."

In my case, that still meant life without the possibility of parole, not the usual sentence for second-degree murder, but my attacker hadn't been the usual victim. Fortunately, despite the Carmichaels' influence, they hadn't been able to charge me with first-degree murder because security vids showed Jaxon's laser pistol falling out of his pocket. But the jury hadn't bought Maridelle's self-defense argument.

8

Excessive force, the prosecution had argued and won. Two weeks after being sentenced to life in prison, I'd been shuttled to the *SS Australia* where a government agent deactivated the electrocuffs, shoved a duffel of my possessions into my arms, and announced I'd been inducted into the Terra-Dakon Goodwill Exchange pilot program.

Or, as I thought of it, Rocks-for-Brides.

"I don't see them rejecting any of us," Andrea said. "They're desperate. They have a critical shortage of women."

Tessa nodded. "An asteroid killed them."

I moved away from the window. "Like the one that hit Earth and killed off the dinosaurs by causing a massive winter that destroyed their food supply?"

"Just like that. The planet is still suffering the winter it triggered," Andrea answered.

"But how would an asteroid strike kill females and not males?"

"They think it carried a virus to which only women were susceptible, and it caused a genetic mutation. Each subsequent generation has produced fewer and fewer females. The planet is 90 percent men now. No worries, though. Everyone who got the virus died a couple of hundred years ago."

9

I gawked in awe. "You had time to research all that?"

She shook her head. "It was in the orientation packet."

I frowned. "Orientation packet?"

"On the little disk," Tessa supplied. "Everyone got one in their cabins."

"Oh, yeah." Vaguely I remembered seeing something like that. I'd found it when I'd boarded the ship but tossed it into a drawer. A depressive fog had engulfed me since the verdict. What difference did anything make? My future was out of my control.

However, Andrea and Tessa had sparked my curiosity. I would pop that disk into the vid player and watch. Horned? I still couldn't get over that. Would the planet resemble Terra? An asteroid-induced winter sounded freezing. It couldn't be that cold, could it? People lived there. Male people, anyway.

Terra had the opposite problem, although not as severe. Women outnumbered men with more than 10 percent more females surviving to adulthood than males. Another reason female convicts were expendable. "Ninety percent men, huh? That's a lot of testosterone."

"I know, right?" Tessa rubbed her arms.

"Assuming they produce testosterone. They might have alien hormones," Andrea pointed out. "In fact, that's pretty much a guarantee seeing how they are aliens."

"But we're still genetically compatible?"

"Theoretically, according to preliminary lab tests. We can't be certain until we start producing children."

Even though I'd been in the grips of an I-was-wrongly-convicted funk, I recalled a couple of blood draws. How could my life have come to this? Sent to a planet light-years away to become an alien's bride. I hugged my midsection. *I gave birth to an alien baby.* It sounded like a story from one of those cheesy 'net vid-zines that focused on celebrity gossip—and sensational news items like my trial.

"I can't believe that the first time we discover intelligent life on another planet, the first action our government takes is trading its female citizens for illuvian ore." Space exploration had discovered alien life a couple of centuries ago in the 2200s, but they were single-celled jelly-like organisms and bacteria. Another planet had had heat-resistant insects, but that was about as advanced as it got.

"Terra One World has been quite civilized compared to what happened the last time Earthers coveted a particular metal ore they deemed valuable," Andrea said.

She meant the quest for gold. A millennium ago, monarch and church-backed explorers decimated native populations in their avarice to acquire the Earth metal. I was aware of our planet's ignominious history, even though I was nowhere near as knowledgeable as Andrea. The woman knew her business, and I suspected, everyone else's. She was sharp—which probably wouldn't serve her well on Dakon. I predicted that having no 'net access would be her biggest adjustment.

"You never ran across a single still or vid that showed what they look like?"

"Not a good one," she said. "There was a still in the orientation vid."

"You couldn't see much because of the fur," Tessa piped up.

"Fur? Good mythological gods, they're furry?" Horns *and* fur?

Tessa and Andrea laughed. "No, they were wearing fur garments with hoods, so you couldn't see their faces clearly," Tessa said. "Just a chin and a nose."

"How did those look?"

Tessa shrugged. "Like a chin and a nose."

"Like a *Terran* chin and nose?"

"Uh huh."

Be thankful for small mercies, anyway. If the dude looked too alien, I would focus on the lower half of his face.

Chapter Two

Torg

I shrugged out of my *kel*, tossed it atop a pile, and sank onto the log bench in front of the fire. After a snowy trek to the meeting place, the blaze warmed my skin.

"Well, how did you do?" Darq asked.

I held up the small round chit I'd drawn from the barrel. "Number three!" I grinned.

"Excellent! You'll get a good pick."

"That's what I figured." I slipped the chit into my carry pouch for safekeeping. The fifty females arriving from a planet called Terra wouldn't be enough for all the unmated men, so we'd held a lottery. The winners, announced yesterday, had drawn chits today to determine the order in which they would choose a female. Being third didn't rate as good as first, but it was more than adequate.

"Have you decided what kind of female you want?" my brother asked.

I'd thought of little else on the way home. Before

yesterday, with little hope of ever mating, I would gladly have accepted any female I could get. Today, with mating assured, I'd gotten picky. I wasn't proud of it, but I couldn't pretend the truth didn't exist.

With so few females, we protected and cosseted the ones we had. They were all special, but given that mine would be an alien, she had to meet some specific requirements. "I need one who is stout and sturdy to weather our winter, whose strong body will produce many offspring, hopefully females."

Darq nodded. "I think that's what everyone would want. The situation is getting dire."

"Our extinction is imminent if we can't acquire mates. The first group of Earth females will be a trial. If it works, the council will arrange for more in exchange for the illuvian ore. The rock is useless to us, but the Terrans are quite interested in it."

Darq snorted. "Crazy aliens."

"Indeed." Council members had joked that the Earth people had rocks for brains, and thought we were getting the better end of the deal, but only time—and female offspring—would prove if they were right.

A healer from the Earth ship had run tests and suggested our two species could reproduce. We had no means to verify that, only their word, but the council of tribal chiefs recognized the exchange program as a last-ditch effort to save our species.

Not everyone agreed, though. The exchange program had its detractors. Many opposed taking alien mates because future generations would be half-breeds, no longer fully Dakonian. Those who preferred survival over extinction, and who were unmated, had entered the lottery. By the luck of the draw, I was chosen, the only one of my tribe.

In my clan of two hundred twelve persons, we had only eighteen adult females and two children, both males, a scenario repeated in other tribes. With each subsequent generation, fewer children were born, and even fewer females. The residual effects of the virus that had arrived with the asteroid two centuries ago continued to plague us. Besides the larger problem of our impending extinction, a lack of mates made men aggressive and irritable. As clan chief, I spent way too much time arbitrating disputes and settling fights.

"Any more rumblings?" I asked.

Darq nodded. "From both sides. Some are appalled you're taking an alien; others are jealous. Mostly the latter." He twisted his mouth wryly. "I wish I could have gotten a female, but the contest was fair."

Though no one dared to say anything to my face,

rumors had spread that I'd been selected for a female because I was chief. Not true. Everyone had had the same chance. At night, I burned with a relentless longing and lust, so I empathized with the feelings of those who'd drawn blanks. But none of them would refuse the opportunity, and I wouldn't either, even if refusal would quell resentment.

I'd been there when the Terran delegation of four males and three females had landed more than four solar rotations ago. We Dakonians were tall, muscular, and strong—even our females. We had to be to survive the harsh climate. Judging from the delegation, Earth people came in a range of sizes. One of the females had been downright puny, child-sized. She wouldn't last a day, let alone a twelve-month winter. Fortunately, they all had dark hair and eyes as we did, so any offspring produced wouldn't look odd. Any female would be a benefit, but I hoped for a strong one. Lottery winners would choose their female in order of their chit. With number three, I stood a good chance of getting what I wanted.

"Why do Terrans think so little of their women they would send them away?" Darq asked.

"It doesn't make sense, does it?" Because we had so few, we treasured our women, protected them, honored them. "But their stupidity is our gain."

I glanced around the dwelling I shared with Darq, trying to view it as an outsider. Would it please my mate? While the snow fell and the wind howled, a roaring fire kept the cave warm and toasty. Wood smoke traveled upward to escape through a hole in the ceiling, scenting the air. Firelight danced on the walls in an ever-shifting artistic display. Kel-hide rugs softened the hard-packed dirt floor. Stacks of hides became comfortable beds. I eyed the pile where I slept. I would have to move it to one of the other chambers to provide my female and I some privacy. It would be cooler, but we would cuddle under the furry hides, and I would keep her warm. Anticipation suffused my body. For the first time in my thirty-four solar rotations, I would have a mate.

"I hope my female will be pleased with her new home."

"How could she not be?" Darq replied. "You're clan chief. You have the largest cave with many rooms, an abundance of kel blankets and rugs. She'll want for nothing." He pointed to the cooking crocks, the pottery, the stone tools. "What more could a female desire?"

I didn't know—that was the problem. Due to the

shortage of females, women could have their pick of mates, and unattached males competed for their attention. Females didn't have to settle. Even being tribal chief hadn't granted me enough of an advantage in the mating pool to attract one—except for Icha, whom I'd never desired. Her sharp personality prompted me to put distance—a lot of distance— between us. I'd tried to let her down easy, but she'd taken it hard when I'd refused her advances.

I surveyed my home. What more could I do to welcome her? "Tomorrow I shall hunt a kel so she'll have fresh meat when she arrives."

Family units shared dwellings, so Darq and I lived in the cave together. In addition, all day long, people of my clan came to me with their problems, their disputes. They sought my advice, my mediation. Other chiefs visited to discuss issues of mutual concern. I was surrounded by people, but in the deepest part of the night, loneliness howled like the wind. Yes, we needed to produce progeny so our people continued, but I longed for a female for personal reasons, too.

"What if she doesn't like me?" I asked.

"Only you would worry so much. Everything will be fine. The day after tomorrow, you will retrieve her, and you'll see."

* * * *

"He stole my female!" Armax shouted.

"I did not," Yorgav denied. "She came willingly. She preferred me to you."

"Liar!"

It took two of my stoutest men to stop them from pummeling each other.

If Armax and Yorgav hadn't bloodied each other already, I would have throttled them myself. I checked the sun's faint glow through the cloud cover. By now, the ship had landed; at this moment, the females were probably disembarking. I should be at the meeting place, but instead, I'd been forced to mediate the dispute between these two. This demonstrated another reason why the exchange program mattered so much. Fighting over females caused more discord than everything else combined. If we had more women, this wouldn't be a problem.

I didn't have time for this today. "Ward them both!"

"But—but..." Both men sputtered.

"Silence!"

Rarely did I consign anyone to the holding caves isolated from the rest of the clan. Disagreements could usually be talked out, but they had picked the wrong day to try my patience. Now I was late; I wouldn't get third pick. Perhaps if Armax and Yorgav chopped firewood for the rest of the clan and slept on the stony ground with a thin kel hide as a covering, they would think twice about fighting in the future.

Protesting, the two men were led away.

"How long do you intend to ward them?" Darq asked. He would keep an eye on matters in my absence.

"Haven't decided yet." Anger burned in the pit of my stomach. I yanked on a heavy coat, snapped the hood over my head then shoved some mittens into the pocket. The coat's outside had been rubbed with kel fat to make it impervious to water, and fur lined the inside. Thankfully, the kel had been one of the animals that had survived the asteroid strike that plunged our planet into winter. Without them, we would have perished. It could still happen if the exchange didn't pan out, if their females could not produce children.

Darq slapped me on the back. "Speed be with you, brother." He understood the stakes.

Fresh snow had fallen overnight, enough to reach the tops of my knee-high boots. I set off at a brisk pace, packing the snow with a heavy stomp. On the return trip, we would walk in the impressions. The woods were still and quiet, my breath, the only sound. My exhalations fogged the air.

As anger dissipated, excitement grew. I'd been wrong to focus on specific requirements. Truth: I would welcome any female who would be mine. I couldn't wait to meet her, the future mother of my daughters and sons, my fireside companion. I expected an adjustment period. We were strangers to one another after all, but I imagined her anticipation to be as great as my own. Why else would she have left her planet to travel among the stars to a new and frozen world?

Soon. Soon. Soon. Soon. The hopeful word repeated in my mind with every step.

•

Chapter Three

Starr

The med tech pressed the muzzle of the medical device behind my right ear. "Hold still."

A sharp pain shot into my head. "Ow!" I slapped the hurting spot. The implant formed a warm, throbbing subdural lump. I shifted my head from side to side. "Is it supposed to feel hot?"

"That goes away."

"How can I tell if the implant is working?"

He shrugged. "If you can understand them, it's working."

"It will automatically translate what I say into their language as well?"

"It sends a signal to the language center of your brain. When you speak to them, it will be in their tongue." He signaled the coordinator. "All done."

I slipped off the stool. We'd been advised that the weather would be "chilly" so we should wear our warmest gear. None of the garments packed by prison personnel were suitable for cold weather, so I'd compensated by donning all the clothing I had with me: two bottoms, two short-sleeved shirts, one long, and, lastly, a knee-length sleep shirt. Multiple layers didn't slim me down any. Would the alien realize my clothing made me look heavier than I was? And why did I care if the alien thought I was fat? I waddled into place beside Andrea and Tessa.

The coordinator raised her hands. "Okay, ladies. This is the moment you've been waiting for. The ship's gangway has lowered. It will be just a little longer before you disembark. When you exit, head directly to the reception center, the large stone pavilion. It's a little nippy out there, so move quickly. Your mates are waiting inside."

My stomach tumbled. I studied the other women to see if they were as nervous as I. This was the first time all of us had been in the same room together and as I surveyed them, it struck me I was the shortest person here. Every single woman had at least seven or eight inches on me, and some were a lot taller than that. At five foot three, I'd gotten used to being one of the shortest people in any gathering, but wasn't it strange nobody stood close to my height? Both Andrea and Tessa were statuesque and muscular, like athletes. About the only thing we had in common physically was our weight. They had me on height, but we probably weighed about the same. They were tall and sleek; I was squat and plump.

Something else I noticed now: how dark the women were. Andrea, like a dozen others, was of Terran African descent. The rest, like Tessa, were Caucasians with dark-brown hair and eyes. Most had permanent chemical tans.

A blued-eyed blonde, I felt like a canary among ravens. *This is a little weird.* What were the odds I'd be the only blonde?

The door slid open, and stewards wheeled in huge carts piled with what appeared to be animal carcasses. "What *is* that?" I clapped a hand over my nose and mouth.

"Animal hide. Fur," Andrea said. "I believe what we smell is called leather."

"It's disgusting."

"People used to cobble shoes and sew clothing out of animal skins."

"But not for hundreds of years." My hand muffled my words. The wealthy bought cotton and linen; the rest of us wore synthetics.

"The Dakonians have provided you with warm coats," the coordinator said. "Form a line, please, and come up and get one."

I would have hung back, but Andrea and Tessa nudged me forward. Grimacing, I accepted the coat, slinging the smelly thing over my arm, holding it away like it was a dead animal. Which it was. Andrea, Tessa, and the other women donned theirs. Giggling, they pulled the hoods over their heads and preened for one another. Gross. How could they stand it?

"How do I look?" Tessa pivoted. The fur covered her from head to knees. She'd done up the wooden toggles that kept it closed. Only her hands, face, and a few strands of brunette hair were visible.

"Like an alien," I said. In the fur, she was indistinguishable from the Dakonian in the orientation video I'd finally watched.

She mimicked horns with her index fingers pressed to her temples. "How about now?"

"Tessa!" Andrea chided, but the corner of her mouth twitched.

Tessa giggled and shoved her hands into some pouches sewn into the sides. She pulled out two hide mitts, the insides lined with fur. "Hey everybody— hand warmers!" She donned them, and the other women checked their pockets and found theirs. Holding the animal hide was bad enough. I had no desire to stick my hand into the skin and rummage around.

"I wonder what kind of animal it was," Tessa mused.

"I believe it is called a kel," the coordinator answered. Pressing a hand to her ear, she cocked her head. "Okay, ladies! We're ready now. Follow me, please." She motioned and exited the conference center.

"This is so exciting! I can't wait to see them." Tessa bounced from foot to foot.

A tornado churned in my stomach at the impending confrontation. Carmichael justice could load me on a shuttle and transport me halfway across the galaxy, but the family couldn't make me copulate with an alien. No way. No how. Not going to happen. If the Dakonians were friendly and pleasant like Terra One World had promised, there should be a getting-to-know-you-hands-off-keep-your-pecker-to-yourself transition period. But, eventually, my so-called mate would expect to get what he'd paid for. The alien was going to be very unhappy.

I only planned to hang out here until my appeal came through. It had to come through. It had to. How Maridelle would notify me, I'd worry about later. *Get through the meet and greet. One thing at a time.*

Single file, we rounded a corner of the ship, and the temperature plummeted at least forty degrees, indicating we neared the gangway. Cold seeped through all my clothing layers. I should have put on the fur. I sniffed. No. The entire corridor reeked from the multiplied effect of forty-nine women covered in dead animals.

I stepped into an icy white world. Needles of cold stung my face and pierced the barrier of clothing like I wore nothing at all. I gasped from the shock of it, drawing frigid air into my lungs.

Hell, that mythological world inhabited by demons wasn't hot at all. It was a frozen, alien wasteland. No wonder Dakonians had horns—they were creatures of the hell they lived in.

Shivers racked my body, and my teeth clattered. Hurriedly, I pulled on the fur. It covered me from neck to ankles. My fingers were so stiff from cold already, I could hardly do up the toggles. I yanked the hood over my head and then dug into the pockets for the mitts. My hands shook so bad, I dropped the mittens in the snow. Before I could retrieve them, the line of women pushed me forward, and the wind swallowed my cry to stop. The cold drew tears from my eyes and froze them on my face.

The only warmth came from a burning hatred for the Carmichaels or Terra One World or whoever had put me here.

Head down, I followed the furry back of the woman in front of me. Andrea? Tessa? I couldn't tell. At least I was in the middle of the pack, so the ones leading the charge had stomped out a path, and my feet didn't get buried in the snow.

A blast of warmth caressed my face. I lifted my head and blinked through the tears at a huge gray stone domed building. The women were entering, holding aside the thick flap of hide serving as a door.

This is it. No backing out now. I choked at my own sad joke. Taking a deep breath, I pushed inside.

Warm. Warm. Warm. Like a mantra, the words rolled through my mind. A large fire blazed in a hearth in the center, the smoke drifting up and out through a hole in the ceiling. Instead of crowding around it, my fellow 'net brides stood still and quiet, staring across the room at...bears. Huge, furry bears.

The aliens.

I'd never seen beings so large, their bulk enhanced by their furs, the hoods thrown back to reveal swarthy faces. My gaze was drawn to their heads. Not a horn in sight. Thick dark straight hair fell to their shoulders. Eyes and ears—thankfully, only two of each. One mouth, one nose. No scales.

Some of them smiled, and I noted with relief they didn't have fangs or lizard-like tongues. Not that I could see.

"They look like Earth men!" whispered a woman on my right, and I realized it was Tessa.

At first glance—yes, but if you focused on the subtleties—no. Working for the Carmichaels I'd learned paying attention kept you alive. If I hadn't caught that slight flicker in Jaxon's eyes, I'd be dead now. So I noticed details others didn't. Dakonian features were craggier, rougher than any Terran male's, their irises so dark they appeared almost black, and while their complexion might be considered "tan" on Earth, it had a tonal quality I'd never seen on a human being. They were way taller than the Terran norm. The shortest one topped seven feet.

"They're hunky," Tessa said.

"Quite nice. They'll do fine," Andrea murmured on my other side.

One woman removed her hood, the others followed suit, and the men's smiles broadened; they liked what they saw. I kept my hood up; I hadn't recovered from the cold. Or maybe I was hiding from seven-foot-tall bogeymen disguised as aliens. Could we trust these men?

One of them broke from the pack and approached. Now I spotted what had been obscured by the distance: little dark-brown nubs poking up out of his hair. They did have horns!

"Welcome, females! I'm Enoki, head of the clan council of Dakon. We are pleased you have arrived."

Females? How wonderfully...objectifying. Or maybe the translation wasn't exact. I rubbed the lump behind my ear. At least I'd understood him; the translator worked.

"Thank you."

"Hello."

"Happy to be here."

The women responded with their own greetings. They did not appear to be offended by being called "female." Anticipation and excitement rose palpably in the room.

"Let me explain how the selection process will work. We were informed fifty of you would arrive in the first phase. To be fair to all unmated men, the council held a lottery. Winners drew a numbered chit. In order, they will choose a mate. If you do not like the man who picks you, you may refuse, and he will choose someone else."

A schoolyard pick? Were they serious? When the rejected man moved on to someone else, woman number two would always remember she'd taken second place. And what about the last woman standing? The men hadn't thought through their little selection process. Still, a part of me warmed to the fact I would have some say-so. For the first time in a long while, I would have input into what happened to me.

The men were still grinning. Their happiness and appreciation seemed genuine—and infectious. Would settling down with an alien be so bad? What did I have waiting for me at home, anyway? My parents had been killed in a hovercraft accident when I was a child; my maternal harpy-of-a-woman grandmother had raised me but never allowed me to forget the depth of her sacrifice. As soon as I was legal, I'd left and never looked back.

But Terra is my home. And it's warm there. I shivered and snuggled deeper into the stinky coat. Was it *always* this cold?

"Once you have agreed to the selection, you will join your mate and travel with him to his camp," Enoki said. "Let us begin. Number one!"

A tall man with black eyes and hair flowing to the hood of his fur—which pretty much described them all—bounded forward. His gaze zeroed in on a pretty woman with olive skin and almond-shaped eyes. Callie, I recalled. Embezzlement. "My name is Krok. I choose you."

Callie smiled, fluttering her lashes. Some people were born flirts. "I would like that."

He held out his hand, and she took it and told him her name. As he led her away, she waved with her free hand. "Bye, ladies! Good luck!"

"Bye, Callie!" We waved.

The farewell hit me with a thud, and I glanced at Tessa and Andrea. We'd become friends. Would we ever see each other again? How far apart were the camps? And what did they mean by camp? That sounded...primitive.

Number two approached Andrea. "You are very beautiful. I'm Groman. I would be honored if you would consent to be my mate."

She sized him up, her scrutiny just shy of a visual rectal exam. For as long as it took her, I almost felt sorry for the guy. I could see his confidence slip with every passing second. Finally, she nodded. "I agree." Andrea grabbed me in a hug. "We'll find a way to meet

35

up," she whispered in my ear. "Remember, his name is Groman."

"Groman," I repeated, hugging her tight. A lump formed in my throat. "I hope you get what you came for, Andrea."

"You, too. Good luck!"

I was looking for my appeal to come through so I could return to Terra.

She embraced Tessa next and then left with her alien beau.

"Number three!" Enoki called.

No one bounded forward. The men glanced at each other. Several checked their chits as if they might have the wrong number.

"Number three?" Enoki called. "Torg?"

"Torg is not here," one man said.

Enoki shook his head. "Very well. He can wait until the end, then. Number four!"

A grinning alien jumped forward.

One by one, women and aliens paired up. Nobody refused anybody. Tessa was chosen tenth by a man named Loka. "Take off your hood so they can see your face," she whispered in my ear when we hugged good-bye.

My chest tightened as she skipped away with her

tall alien squeeze. They reminded me of newlyweds.
The only thing this party lacked was confetti. And
cake. I wished I had some. The selection process had
triggered an urge to stress eat. Out of fifty women,
Andrea had been chosen second and Tessa tenth. An
irrational jealousy knotted my stomach, and the
beginnings of humiliation heated my face.

Eleven. Twelve. Thirteen. Fourteen. Taking
Tessa's advice, I pushed off the hood. Twenty-five,
twenty-six. Not a single alien glanced in my direction.
Thirty-one. Thirty-two. I was no raving beauty, but I
rated on par with at least *some* of the remaining
women. I had nice eyes. Good skin. A cute nose. Sure, I
carried excess baggage around my hips and thighs, but
in the disgusting, smelly fur they couldn't tell! We were
all bulky blobs. What was wrong with these aliens?
Forty-five. I crossed my arms, tucked my still-freezing
hands under my armpits, and glowered. Fine.

Forty-seven, forty-eight.

Last one. Forty-nine strode up to the other woman
not chosen. "I'm so relieved," he said. "I worried
someone else would claim you before my number
came up. Would you be my mate?"

Smarmy asshat. My throat thickened, and I
yanked the hood over my head. If I could have crawled

into a snowdrift, I would have. These aliens, desperate for women, had passed me over—every single one of them. I huddled in my fur and pressed my tongue to the roof of my mouth to keep from crying. Only me and Enoki, the head alien, remained.

He cleared his throat. "By default, Torg will be yours."

I'd forgotten about missing number three. It didn't matter because nobody had chosen me; no one had looked at me. Why?

"I cannot imagine what is keeping Torg," Enoki said.

A blast of cold air shot into the room as the flap lifted. "I'm here!"

Chapter Four

Torg

A multitude of double sets of footprints led away from the meeting place; most, if not all the choosing had already been done. Fury ignited anew. The thaw would come before Armax and Yorgav got out of the warding cave.

I hurried to the lodge, pushed aside the flap, and entered. "I'm here!"

Enoki faced a lone figure wrapped in kel. Tiny, hardly bigger than a child. I hoped first impressions were deceiving.

"You're late! You have been disrespectful." The council chief glared at me over the woman's bowed head. No, she was as little as she appeared to be.

"A problem occurred in camp. I apologize for my tardiness."

"It is not me you should apologize to. Torg, meet your mate."

The woman turned. Yellow straw like the grasses that fed the kel before the onslaught of winter stuck out from beneath a hood that hid half her face. From the little I could see, she had a tiny chin, well-shaped lips, and a button nose stung pink from the cold. She raised her head and pushed back the hood.

I tried not to recoil, but shock shot through me. The straw covered her entire head! It sprang from her scalp in loose spirals, curling around her neck and brushing her shoulders. Just as shocking, her eyes were blue like the sky during our too-short growing season, an unnatural and disconcerting color to see on a person.

Worse, she was scrawny. Her head didn't reach my shoulder, and even with the added bulk of the thick kel, I could tell she was skin and bones. I'd hoped for a female who resembled a Dakonian but had gotten one who couldn't have looked more alien if she'd tried.

But she was mine. I had a mate! Satisfaction and possessiveness I'd never experienced filled me in a rush, and in a flash I understood why the two men in the warding cave had fought over the female. I would fight anyone who would take this one from me.

Even if she wasn't quite what I would have chosen.

Even if she did glare at me with dislike.

I couldn't blame her. I had disrespected her with my tardiness. I approached. "I am sorry for my lateness. My name is Torg."

She remained silent. Was the translator malfunctioning? Had she had one implanted at all? The Terrans had promised to take care of that.

"*Starrconner*." Her voice was low, husky voice, and despite her alienness, I felt an immediate quickening in my groin.

"Starrconner." I repeated the unusual name to ensure I got it right.

"*Juststarr*," she said.

"Juststarr?"

"Call. Me. Starr." She pointed to the ceiling. "Star. Like what's in the sky at night."

"Starr," I tried again.

"That's right."

"We must go now. It is a bit of a walk, and it will be night soon." The brightness of the snow amplified the starlight, providing more than enough illumination to see, but the temperature dropped precipitously once darkness fell. And if the winds kicked up... Despite her kel, Starr appeared cold already. Plus, I was eager to take her home. *My mate*. How incredible that sounded.

"Walk? Out there? How far?"

"Approximately two *tripta*."

41

She did not react at first, and then she clapped a hand behind her ear, and her eyes widened. "A tripta is almost five *kilometers*. Two tripta is nine and a half kilometers. In the snow?"

"Kilometer? I don't recognize that word. A tripta is the distance a man walking at a steady pace can cover in one hour." Rushing, I'd completed the trip in much less time, but I didn't expect my female could travel that fast. "We're fortunate. My camp is close to the meeting place. Others came from much farther away."

Enoki nodded in confirmation.

"You don't have any kind of transport? No hovercraft? Ground vehicles?" She tugged the fur around her neck.

"We have wagons on skis," I replied. "They are pulled by kel, but the animals can be only partly domesticated, so they are unpredictable and bolt without warning. We limit wagon use to transporting materials, not people."

"You use animals?"

"What else would you use?"

"Oh, I don't know...illuvian ore?"

"Rocks? What would we do with rocks?"

"Okay, energy cells. Solar power. Hell, even fossil fuel or steam."

I shook my head. "We have none of that anymore."

"Good gods. I've been transported to the Stone Age."

Once our lives had been different, but then the asteroid changed everything. For two centuries, we'd clung to survival and had been about to lose our grip when the Terrans showed up. Fifty females wouldn't be enough to save us, but it was a start. And if more arrived...

I glanced at my undersized female with the yellow straw hair and eerie eyes. She represented our last hope. Our children would be only half Dakonian, but half was better than none.

"You should be on your way," Enoki urged, "before night falls and brings greater cold. You do not wish for your female to grow chilled."

I knew that! It irked me that he had felt the need to point it out like I'd been derelict in my duty to care for her. I did not like the way he smiled at her, either. Or the way she responded. If she smiled at anyone, it should be me.

"Let's go. Follow me," I said tersely, and then noticed her bare hands. "Don't you have mittens?"

"I lost them."

"Take mine." I dug out my set.

She slipped them on. They were so large on her she could have put two hands in one mitten.

The cold snapped at my face when I held the flap open for Starrconner to exit. With a brisk pace, I led the way across the compound, the snow packed to icy hardness from people treading over it. The sooner we arrived at camp and our cave, the sooner she and I could get to know each other.

"Oh-oh...crap!" *Thud.*

I whipped around. Starrconner lay flat on her back. "*Motherfucker...son of a bitch.*" From her tone, I surmised the unfamiliar words were curses. I rushed to her side and assisted her to her feet.

"Are you all right?"

"The ground is slicker than dog snot." She pushed off the hood and rubbed her head.

I didn't know what dog snot was, but I understood slick. I pointed toward the woods. "We'll go that way. Walk in my footsteps, and it will be easier for you." I brushed the snow from her coat, flipped the hood over her head, and tucked wayward strands of hair inside. Though it resembled straw, it felt very soft, slippery in a good way, and I had to resist grabbing a handful and stroking it. It was too soon for such personal contact.

But maybe a compliment would break the ice? "Your hair is slicker than dog snot." I tried an idiom from her language.

Her jaw dropped, and then she scowled at me before stomping toward the woods, and I realized I must have said the wrong thing. The translator left a lot to be desired. If it was an example of advanced Terran technology, it did not appear to be all that helpful.

I raced in front so I could lead the way. I located my indentations in the snow and stepped into them. The hike was easygoing, and I moved quickly, but when I checked on Starr, she'd fallen behind. So much smaller than I, she struggled to reach the holes I'd left for her. My footsteps were too far apart for her short stride, and the snow was too deep. Where it came up to my shins, it banked around her thighs. Her kel, dragging through the snow, hindered her progress further.

I retraced my steps, planting a deep footprint in between the original ones.

"How long is your winter?" she asked.

"Twelve months," I replied.

"The whole year?" She looked horrified.

"There are fifteen months in our year. In two

centuries, our winter has gradually receded. When the asteroid first hit, we did not see sunlight for years," I explained. "That was long before I was born."

She tilted her head. "How old are you, Torg?" It was the first time she'd addressed me by name. Spoken in her husky Terran accent, it sounded alien and oddly arousing.

"Thirty-four annual rotations. You?"

"Twenty-eight."

Now I knew two facts about my female. Her name and her age. *Starrconner* was twenty-eight rotations.

"What are the other three months like?"

"Warmer. The snow melts. Grasses grow, and flowers bloom almost overnight. That is our growing season when we plant and then harvest and prepare for the cold. How many months of winter does your planet have?"

"By the calendar, three, but the length and intensity vary. Some places get very cold like this, and winter lasts five or six months. Other places are tropical and don't get cold at all. But, usually, winter is three months."

"I think I would like a short winter."

"Yeah, I didn't appreciate the shortness."

I wondered why she'd come if there were plenty of

men on Terra and the climate was so nice, but that discussion would be better in front of a warm fire. "Let's proceed." Most of our trek lay ahead of us. "I should carry you."

"No. No, I can walk. Just...go slower and try not to take such big steps."

"I can do that." I nodded.

This time, I made fresh tracks, stepping between the ones I'd left on the way to the meeting place, so they would be closer together for her. Still, progress was slow. Every time I checked on her, she seemed to be struggling but refused my many offers to carry her.

My kel and fur boots held the outside chill at bay, while the satisfaction of having a female filled me with inner warmth. Many times I'd trekked to the meeting place, sometimes with Darq or other men, but never had I felt the degree of companionship I did with Starr, even though we didn't speak. Already I regretted my initial reaction to her appearance. Her yellow-straw hair, while unsightly, was as soft as baby kel fuzz. I did wish for her sake she was bigger, had more padding on her, because she would have an easier time with our winter, but her skinniness didn't affect my growing attachment.

Perhaps Armax and Yorgav deserved my thanks.

Had I arrived on time, I would not have chosen Starr, and then I would not have known this satisfaction. However, I couldn't *unward* them prematurely. They needed to learn fighting didn't resolve differences. The climate provided enough of a challenge without us battling each other. Discord consumed energy and resources we needed for survival, and even the new arrivals did not assure our future. Dissension threatened us all. Dakonians had a long, hard hike before we could rest. The female shortage would not resolve itself for at least a generation or two.

But, now that I had a female of my own, I empathized with Armax. If anyone tried to steal Starr from me, I might react as he had. Perhaps I should be more lenient.

In the stillness of the wood, I became aware of an odd sort of clattering. I stopped and cocked an ear. "Do you hear that?"

"W-w-what-t-t?" Starr asked.

I whipped around. Her teeth were knocking together, and her entire body shook with the shivers. I stomped the few paces toward her. "You're freezing!"

"H-h-hell, y-y-eah!" Her tone implied my comment had been ridiculous.

"The kel should have kept you warm."

"The c-c-coat is fine, but my feet are w-w-wet. We don't have much f-f-farther to go, right? We're almost th-th-there?"

Her flimsy footwear! Why hadn't I brought her some warm kel boots? The Terrans might be able to travel across the galaxy in flying ships, but they didn't know snowballs about how to dress in the cold. I should have predicted this and been better prepared. That's why the council had collected and provided the kel—just in case. And they'd been right.

Had we been able to walk at my pace, we would have been home already. "We have traveled half the distance."

"Oh g-g-gods." She looked ready to cry.

Enough. Sometimes a man had to do what was right despite what his female said. I bent, scooped her up, and slung her over my shoulder.

"No! S-s-stop! P-p-put me down!"

Snow clung to her from feet to mid-thigh. The thin leggings covering her limbs were wet and stiff with ice. Cold could be deadly to the insufficiently insulated. I hurried, jogging now that I didn't have to slow my pace.

Dangling over my shoulder, she struck at my buttocks and legs, her pats ineffectual through my

49

thick kel. The exertion would assist in warming her.

"Your protests would carry more weight if you could utter them without your teeth chattering."

"I'm t-t-too heavy for you to carry all that way."

She weighed scarcely more than a snowflake. "Ha! You make a joke. I like that my female has a sense of humor."

Chapter Five

Starr

Torg's shoulder dug into my stomach like a rock. A broad, hard, masculine rock. He loped through the snow at a speed I couldn't have matched on my best day in the fairest weather. My toes hurt from the cold, and I couldn't stop shivering, but I hammered at his backside to get him to put me down. Although being slung over his shoulder like a sack of genetically engineered potatoes did lessen the intimacy, the close contact disturbed me for many reasons: despite his seeming ease at carrying me, I *was* too heavy; I'd made a point of standing on my own two feet; I wasn't sure I wanted to go where he was taking me; and he'd turned out to be nothing like what I'd expected.

His barbarian chivalry was making me like him.

Not part of the plan. I had to go back. Besides, chemistry *mattered.* A guy should be so besotted he tripped over his own feet. Torg wasn't. He bounded through the snow like a gazelle or a kel or whatever. Yeah, yeah, we'd only met a couple of hours ago. But

I'd seen disappointment in his eyes at the lodge dome place. Shock at first sight. He'd masked it, and he'd treated me courteously since then, but I couldn't forget. If he hadn't arrived late and been stuck with me, he wouldn't have chosen me, either. On a planet desperate for women, not a single alien picked me.

I'd been told I had pretty eyes—striking, most people said—and I'd secretly thought I had nice hair, so it had to be my weight. Aliens didn't take to curvy girls. What else could it be?

"Put me down." I punctuated another token protest with a light slap.

If he complied, I'd be in trouble. My cheap synth shoes offered little protection or warmth. Water had soaked through them. Wearing them was little better than going barefoot. Needles of pain stabbed at my toes and feet. My legs had gone numb. Without the coats, we would have perished from hypothermia. I wondered how Andrea and Tessa were faring.

"Not until we get to camp," he replied to my relief.

The continued "camp" reference worried me. I hoped the implant had mistranslated. On Terra One World, people spent days or weeks in wilderness areas called camps for the sole purpose of making their lives difficult. They called it "roughing it." You slept on the hard ground in makeshift, inadequate shelters. It was dirty and dusty. You were either too hot or too cold. Insects bit you. If it rained, you got wet. And that was on a civilized, advanced planet.

Roughing it on Dakon? I shuddered.

"We'll be home soon." Torg must have read my mind.

"Tell me about your home," I said. "What is it like?"

"It is one of the nicest tribal camps. Other clans would claim it in a heartbeat if they could. The caves provide natural shelters and are much better than anything manmade."

"Did you say cave? A hollowed-out chamber in the rock?"

"That's right. But there are many tunnels going deep into the mountainside."

More than a straw that broke the camel's back, this was the log that crushed the animal and finished it off. I'd been falsely convicted of a crime, exiled to a frozen remote planet, preventing me from participating in my appeal, wrapped in a stinky animal skin, handed over to an alien who'd found me lacking—and *now* I had to live in a *cave* during an eternal winter?

Since I hung upside down, the tears trickling from my eyes froze on my forehead. I cried harder. Uncontrollable sobs shook my body. Not only was I fat, ugly, and weak, I'd been reduced to a basket case.

"Starrconner, what is wrong?" Torg stopped and slid me off his shoulder. Instantly I missed his body heat.

"N-n-nothing," I stuttered.

His frown held concern and confusion. "Your translator must not be working. *This*"— he gestured at my tears—"does not mean nothing. Why are you crying?"

"Because." It was all too much.

But mostly, for some strange reason, I wanted him to like me—and I didn't want to live in a cave.

A touch to my shoulder became an awkward pat, and then I found myself enveloped in an alien bear hug, my face pressed to Torg's massive chest, covered by the animal hide. It stank, but *he* smelled good. And felt good. Rock solid. Like the kind of man you could lean on. For so long, I'd had only myself to rely on.

I hiccupped and sniffed, trying to suck back the snot. From his pouch, Torg withdrew a swatch of, what else, animal hide, and dabbed at my face. "It will be all right, *Starrconner*. I promise."

The blending of my first and last name into one showed he still didn't understand Terran naming structures, but in his rough, gravelly alien voice, it sounded so sweet and so charming, I cried harder. In another time, in another place, I might have wanted him. Maybe I did anyway.

No, I didn't. I planned to clear my name, go home where I had real buildings, transportation, and the 'net, and resume my regularly scheduled life free of the Carmichaels.

Didn't I?

Torg scooped me up, but rather than sling me over his shoulder, he carried me cradled in his arms.

* * * *

I could have walked in, but Torg had to duck to enter the cave, and as soon as he did, the temperature jumped, warming more as he moved farther into a cavern lit by flaming torches. Our shadow, huge and hulking, crept along stony walls as we burrowed deeper. He hadn't been kidding about the tunnel. "You can put me down, now."

"Not yet." He tightened his arms.

A second shadow appeared and then a big brute of man came into view. Dark hair fell to his shoulders. He resembled Torg, although younger and less handsome.

"I expected you much earlier. You're late."

Torg's mouth twisted. "My usual state these days."

"I was getting worried."

"I'm fine, although my female got chilled." His possessive, yet objective phrasing should have irked me, but it didn't. Maybe he liked me a little? "Do me a favor and move a bed close to the fire, will you?"

"Already did," he answered. "And I have a pot of stew cooking."

"You think of everything. Thank you. This is my female, Starconner, although she prefers to be called Starr." Torg met my gaze. "This is my brother, Darq."

"I'm very pleased to meet you, Starr." Darq smiled.

"It's nice to meet you, too," I replied.

Torg jutted his head. "Lead the way."

Darq reversed and headed down the passage from which he'd come. He was shorter than Torg, but both men ducked to enter a low opening into a chamber. Inside was so toasty, I had to stifle a moan of pleasure. More torches lit the room, and a fire crackled in a large pit ringed by stone. Something delicious bubbled in a clay pot set over glowing coals. Smoke spiraled upward and out through an opening in the rocky ceiling. As primitive as I'd feared, it was *warm* and surprisingly

56

homey.

Torg lowered me to a pile of furs near the fire. "We need to get you out of those wet clothes," he said, and divested himself of his own coat. The removal of the bulky outerwear should have diminished him, but instead it enhanced his size. The breadth of his muscled shoulders could have supported two of me! A broad chest tapered to a flat abdomen and slim hips. A leather tunic and pants molded to his body like a glove, calling my attention to the bulge between his muscular thighs. Impressive, and he wasn't even hard. I gulped, recalling the conversation with Andrea and Tessa about the aliens' junk.

He knelt beside me and tugged at my fur. "If you take this off, you'll feel the heat better," he coaxed with a smile.

Oh, I felt the heat.

Good gods he was attractive. A scruff of dark beard tinged his face and whitened his already-bright and slightly crooked smile. He had full lips, and, just above and to the left of them, a small devilish scar. Thick, shiny hair dusted his wide shoulders. And, poking through the thick strands, two brownish nubs. Horns. About as cute as cute could be.

"Starr? You should take off the kel," he repeated.

"Oh, right." I shook off the borrowed mittens, but my fingers couldn't seem to work the toggles. How was it possible to be frozen and flushed at the same time?

"Let me help you." He brushed my fingers aside, undid the kel, and slipped it off my shoulders. "You're soaked!" he exclaimed.

The synthetic fiber of my clothing had wicked up the moisture so that even the parts not exposed to the elements had gotten wet.

"I'll get her some dry clothes." Darq disappeared to return moments later and toss a garment to Torg. "One of your tunics."

"I did not think to order any garments in her size, not that I would have guessed right. Tomorrow, we will get some from the tanner."

"Children's clothing would fit her best," Darq suggested.

"I think you're right."

"Children's?" I sputtered.

"You are much smaller than our own females. Adult sizes would be way too large for you." He reached for the hem of my sodden nightshirt.

"No." I pulled away. I glanced between Torg and Darq.

"What's wrong?"

"I can't take my clothes off in front of you."

"Why not?"

"Because we just met! I hardly know you, and I don't know your brother at all!"

"What does that have to do with removing your wet clothing?"

"Do you strip naked in front of anybody?"

"If our clothes get wet, and we are chilled, we remove them. It only makes sense." Torg glanced at his brother, who shrugged as if to say, "You got me." We'd run into one of those cultural differences.

"Not to me." I snatched up one of the lighter furs and covered myself, feeling exposed enough under their scrutiny. I doubted I'd ever be ready to reveal my nudity to Torg of the perfect body, and certainly not to his bystander brother who wasn't involved in this mating deal. Did all Dakonians live with siblings and or families? Darq had kept the fire going, had prepared the meal I hoped would be served soon, and had trotted off to get me dry clothing. He seemed to defer to Torg. Was that typical younger sibling behavior?

"We must remove your footwear, at least," Torg said. "I must check for frostbite."

"That you can do," I replied, and allowed him to tug off one of my ankle-high shoes.

59

Torg peered at it. The synthetic material supposedly made it impervious to water, but that had proven to be a crock. I hadn't gone a half kilometer before the shoes had soaked through. His sexy mouth curled with disgust, and he tossed the shoe aside. "Those are worthless."

Agreed. If he hadn't carried me, I would have been in deep Dakonian doo-doo.

He dispensed with the other shoe in a similar manner then peeled off my two pairs of socks. With his strong, gentle hands he massaged my feet. "Your toes are like ice."

Never in a million years would I have expected to have a hunky, sexy alien tending to me, massaging my feet. Unfortunately, it hurt too much to enjoy it. Needlelike jabs of sensation stabbed at my toes, intensifying as my feet warmed.

"Ow, ow." I grimaced and fell onto my elbows.

"I know it hurts. It will get better." He peered at a foot. "You're fortunate you didn't suffer permanent damage." He glanced at Darq. "Be sure to get her a pair of boots as well as clothing."

About the time pain turned to pleasure, he stopped the massage. "Now, your garments."

I shook my head.

"You're cold and wet. You'll be much warmer in dry clothes."

For sure, but undressing in front of them would not happen. "No."

He raked a hand over his head. Despite the circumstances and our standoff, I wondered how his hair would feel between my fingers. It looked so smooth and shiny. No man should have hair that nice. It wasn't right. "You're my female. It's my job to take care of you. I'm not going to give in on this." Sexy brown eyes hardened.

I pulled the kel closer to my chin then got an idea. "I'll change clothes under the blanket." Waiting for my sodden clothes to dry on my body didn't appeal to me, either.

"All right." He passed over the tunic Darq had retrieved.

Wiggling out of multiple layers underneath a heavy animal hide took a while. Torg's amazement grew with each garment that I handed him. Finally naked from the waist up, I yanked on the tunic, my haste fueled more by habit than fear. I was alone in a cave billions of miles from home with a strange alien, but I was starting to trust him. If he had intended to attack me, he would have done it already.

The tunic, sewn from a soft and supple hide, was warm against my skin. I was getting used to the kel smell; it didn't bother me as much as it had at first. Modesty secured, I worked on removing clothing from my lower half.

Sodden pants and leggings resisted efforts to peel them off, but I succeeded. My topmost pants had deep pockets on the hips and legs, and into them I'd stuffed my extra underwear.

A pair of briefs fell out of a pocket.

Torg picked it up and rubbed the fabric between his fingers. Caressed it. "What is this?"

Oh great. Now I had an alien fondling my underwear. The best thing to do would be to act natural and unconcerned, but heat flooded my face, and I grabbed the panties and shoved them back into a pocket. "Underwear," I mumbled.

"You wear them under your clothing?"

"Yes."

"For what reason?"

To provide extra warmth or to stimulate sexual interest didn't apply here, and no way was I going to discuss the utilitarian, hygienic purpose for underwear. "It's something Terrans do."

He accepted that explanation with a nod.

"Don't you wear underwear?" It took all my willpower to refrain from checking out his bulge.

"No."

"Why not?"

"It is something Dakonians don't do." His amused grin shot straight to my erogenous zones. Another smile like that and the evidence would show why we wore briefs. I pressed my legs together. Torg rose to his feet and hung my wet clothing over a rack near the fire.

Darq cleared his throat. I'd forgotten he was here. "If you have your female settled, a serious matter requires your attention."

"What is it?"

"While you were gone, Armax tried to kill Yorgav."

Torg's curse didn't need a translation. "How? They were warded! Surely they weren't put in the same chamber together?"

Darq shook his head. "No, but jealousy and anger exceeded honor. Armax left his warding chamber, sought out Yorgav, and attacked him while he slept. Yorgav may not survive."

"Armax must be banished."

Banishment didn't sound good. Having experienced the climate up close and personal, I couldn't imagine being alone out there. I would have frozen to death if not for Torg. Without being told, I knew on a world like this one, numbers provided protection. We'd arrived at camp to a crackling fire and a bubbling dinner because another person had been involved.

"I feared you'd say that," Darq said. "We're in the worst part of winter."

"What would you have me do?" Torg asked. "We cannot allow that level of violence. I won't have a murderer in our tribe. Banishment is the only solution."

Guilt and fear lodged in my throat in a choking lump. On the *SS Australia* we'd been open, even boastful of our crimes. Of course, I was innocent. But would Torg believe me when all the "evidence" contradicted me? I'd been convicted; a court of my peers bought or blackmailed by the Carmichaels had certified my alleged guilt. Would Torg banish *me* if he found out? In effect, I'd already been exiled once— Terra One World had shipped me to Dakon. But to be kicked out of the safety of the tribe into a frozen wilderness?

How many people had I told of my conviction? I racked my brain. Andrea and Tessa for sure. How many would they tell? To my knowledge, I was the only one aboard the *SS Australia* who'd been convicted of a *violent* crime. The rest had been white collar and/or property crimes. A safe bet on Terra's part. Dakon had nothing to steal. From what I could see, they didn't have anything of value other than the illuvian ore—which Terra had dibs on—and maybe stinky kel furs. The jury was still out on those.

"You're right, and you're clan chief," Darq said. "It is your decision."

Torg was clan chief? No wonder his brother deferred to him.

"W-what if, uh, Armax didn't do it?" I asked.

Darq replied, "He did it. Yorgav's blood stained Armax's hands and tunic."

I'd been splattered with Jaxon Carmichael's blood after I cracked his head open. "But if Armax is banished, he could die out there, right?" I pictured my cold, frozen body buried in the snow. When the growing season came, I'd still be there—perfectly preserved in ice.

"He could." Torg nodded. "Unless he can convince another clan to take him in." He looked at Darq. "My female has a soft heart. Expel him, but give him an extra kel hide."

Darq nodded. "What about Icha?"

"She stays. We cannot afford to lose a female. Besides, she has made her choice, has she not?"

"I'm not sure if she chose Yorgav over Armax, or if she was trying to make him jealous."

"Icha has been a troublemaker since she was a girl, but the clan still needs her."

"What if Yorgav dies?"

"Then she will choose another mate."

Chapter Six

Torg

My female's stomach rumbled. She grimaced. "Sorry."

"You shouldn't apologize for being hungry," I said. "I'm the one who should apologize." I'd forgotten about feeding her. I hurried to the simmering stew Darq had prepared, ladled a generous portion into a wooden bowl, and brought it to her with a wooden spoon. Hearty meals would fatten her up. I accepted her the way she was, but if she gained more weight she'd weather our freezing climate better.

She stared into the bowl. "Is this kel?"

"And some dried root vegetables that have been rehydrated. How did you know?" I asked.

She looked so adorable cuddled up in the hide, her yellow hair curling around her face, clutching the bowl in her two tiny hands. But for Armax and Yorgav, I would have passed her over, and that would have been terrible. I owed them a debt of gratitude. Curses on Armax for taking the dispute to the next level and forcing me to enforce the law. Our survival depended on order, on us working together. Fighting among ourselves would destroy us faster than any freezing temperature ever could. Murder was the ultimate taboo. Aggression ran high, and men fought, but in my lifetime there hadn't been a homicide.

"Lucky guess," she said. "Aren't you going to eat?"

"Soon." Darq signaled he wanted to speak to me alone. "I'll be right back."

I followed my brother deeper into the tunnel where our voices wouldn't be overheard.

"You seem very pleased with your female," he said.

"I am."

"She is...*different* from what I expected. Her hair and eyes are most unusual. Very alien."

"Her features are starting to grow on me."

"Did the others look like her?" He waved his hands. "The yellow...the eyes..."

I shrugged. "I arrived too late to see them. The others had been chosen. Enoki was displeased with me, but I'm happy it worked out the way it did. I don't want anyone making her feel bad for her appearance." I narrowed my eyes. "Including you." Including myself. I felt ashamed of my initial disappointment.

"I would never do that."

68

"Good."

"While you were gone, a council messenger came to the camp," Darq said. "The Terrans intend to set up a communication center at the meeting place so our two peoples can better conduct business. They have something called a 'net. It allows you to talk over long distances. In exchange for more ore, they will expedite the shipment of more females."

Armax and Yorgav, a communications center, more females. I'd only been gone for six hours. "Much happened in my absence." Surprising Enoki hadn't mentioned it, but then he'd been annoyed with me. For good reason. I shouldn't have kept my mate waiting.

"I'm considering entering the lottery."

"That's an excellent idea." I clapped him on the shoulder. "I wish you to be as fortunate as I am."

"But…" He fidgeted.

"You don't like the Terrans' appearance." Anger in defense of Starr kindled in the pit of my stomach.

"That's not it at all. Forget I said anything. I'm sure it's just jealousy. You should go back to your female." Darq turned to leave.

"Hold it." I barred his path. "What do you mean, jealousy?"

"It's nothing. A rumor."

"Now I need to know."

He sighed. "The messenger told me he'd heard gossip in another camp that the females sent were problems."

"Problems? What does that mean?"

"That they had broken Terran laws and were given the choice of being warded or coming here."

"That's ridiculous! If that were true, I would have heard." As clan chief, I rotated on a council seat. Enoki would have told me.

Unless Enoki didn't know. The females had just arrived.

Why *had* they left their planet to fly across the galaxy to become mates of men they'd never met? To leave their advanced, warm planet for a challenging existence on a frozen alien one?

Starr couldn't have done anything wrong. I didn't know her well, but my gut voted for innocence. We hadn't gotten off to a great start, but since then I'd sensed a bond growing between us. The rumor couldn't be true.

But I would ask her about it to prove to Darq and anyone else that it was false.

* * * *

Starr peered up as I entered the main room. Relief

flashed in her eyes, and if I wasn't mistaken, welcome. She was glad to see me. A pleasurable warmth filled my chest along with the conviction Darq was wrong. I put the rumor out of my head to enjoy her smile. Her empty bowl rested on the floor.

"Everything okay?" she asked.

Yes, because the rumor was baseless. Men jealous at not winning a female tried to spoil it for the rest. "Just fine. Are you still hungry? Would you like more to eat?" I asked.

"I shouldn't, but...yes. It was delicious."

"Why shouldn't you?" I refilled her bowl and got one for myself. I settled next to her on the kel. We would sleep here tonight. The other chambers were heated by small fires, but they weren't this warm. Once she acclimated to our winter, we could move where we would have more privacy.

She lifted a shoulder. "I shouldn't eat so much. Where is your brother? Will he be joining us?"

Not if he knew what was good for him. "His chamber is a bit deeper in the cave. He has retired there."

"I'm glad," she said, and then clapped a hand over her mouth. "That didn't come out the way I had intended. He did all of this." She waved her hands at

71

the stew pot, the pile of kel. "He seemed nice...I should shut up now."

I chuckled. "I know what you meant." If Darq hadn't made himself scarce, I would have suggested it. I desired to be alone with her. That she wanted the same was a good sign.

I couldn't believe my good fortune. I was sitting here on my furs with my mate! Starr was everything I'd longed for. There was so much I needed to say to her—yet the words fell away.

Flames snapped and crackled, throwing shadows of two figures on the wall. For so long, there'd only been one. Now there were two. I had my brother, and I was surrounded by others in my camp, but their company couldn't compare. My dream had come true, and I could think of nothing to say? Like a fool, I shoveled stew into my mouth as silence swelled.

She glanced around the cave. "This is cozy. Much warmer than I thought it would be."

"Yes!" I agreed. "It is warm."

"If not for you, I would have died out there."

"I wouldn't have let that happen."

"You said most other Dakon do not live in caves. What do they live in?"

"Stone huts."

"Like the meeting place?"

"Yes, like that. Only smaller. And huts are shared because digging stone is hard work and the growing season is so short."

"Are the different clans spaced very far apart?"

"One to four tripta from one to the next."

Her face fell. "Pretty far, then."

"Not so far," I corrected her. "We traveled two tripta to get here."

Her shoulders slumped.

"That's a concern for you? Why?"

"My friends are at other camps. I had hoped to visit them sometime."

"I will see that you visit them." Anything to ensure her happiness. "What are their names? Do you know who they were paired with?"

Her eyes brightened. "Andrea and Tessa. Andrea went with a man named Groman, and Tessa was chosen by Loka."

"I'm familiar with both of them. Their camps are not that far. Loka's is closest to the meeting place. We'll go for a visit soon."

"Thank you!" Her eyes glowed, and my chest swelled with pleasure at the way she was looking at me. Like I'd done something special.

"I'm a clan chief." I wasn't boasting but minimizing. "It's a small matter." My heart hammered in my chest as I reached over and covered her hand, warm now but no less small and delicate. When she did not pull away, the thudding in my chest increased.

"It's not a small matter to me," she said softly. She raised herself up onto her knees and then leaned in very close to me and brushed her lips against my mouth. I widened my eyes as the unfamiliar touch reverberated through my body.

She sat down again, as calm and still as could be, while sensations and emotions careened inside me.

"How many people are in your clan?" she asked.

"Just over two hundred."

"Are the other clans the same size?"

"A few are smaller, some are larger, perhaps five hundred or so."

"And there are how many clans?"

"Fifteen."

"That can't be all the people on your planet?"

"You know about the asteroid?"

She nodded.

"It killed millions, and the winter that followed killed millions more. And animals. Many species are now extinct. The clans are the descendants of the survivors who found each other and banded together. It is possible descendants of other survivors live on the far side of Dakon, but we have no way of finding out. It is too far to travel by foot. The strike flattened every structure to rubble, caused fires that burned for decades, and released so much dust and smoke into the air it caused a climate change.

"At first, winter had no end and our people fought to survive. Now we have three months of sunny weather we call the growing season, and we gain about one day per year. During the growing season, we send explorers to search for other people, but time and distance limit how far they can go. They have to be back before winter comes again.

"We never traveled among the stars like your people, but we weren't always this primitive. We had big cities and vehicles that flew through the air. We lost all that."

"You couldn't rebuild?"

"With what? We lost infrastructure, tools, and the people with the knowledge. You traveled here on a spaceship, did you not?"

"Yes."

"Explain how you build a spaceship."

"Robots do that in factories."

"The factory and the robots have been demolished."

"You build more robots."

"The parts and machinery to build robots have been destroyed. And where are the instructions to build the parts?"

"In databases."

"Which have been wiped out."

"Oh."

"The asteroid strike transported us to an elemental, basic existence. We were forced to start over." I smoothed my hand over one of the hides. "Fortunately, the kel survived. They provide us with food, clothes, and tools. We use the skin, the meat, the antlers, the bones. No part of the animal is wasted. Without them, none of us would have survived."

"You have illuvian ore."

"Which we use." I paused. "Remember the meeting place? The stone walls..."

She widened her eyes. "You build your structures out of it? But it's useful for so much more...transmitters, energy cells, it's a natural electromagnetic conductor..."

"We don't have the knowledge to use it in that manner. Or, if we ever did, it was lost when the asteroid hit. But we found another good use for the ore."

"What?" she asked, but then realization dawned and she flushed.

"Yes, that." Ore became the currency that we used to buy females.

I sought her gaze. "Why did you come, Starr? Why did you fly across the galaxy to a planet as primitive as this when you had plenty of potential mates on your planet?"

Chapter Seven

Starr

I'd been expecting the question, but not this soon, so I had no answer prepared. In the depths of Torg's fierce, piercing gaze, vulnerability and earnestness glinted. He deserved the truth, but the truth would hurt him and endanger my safety, and I couldn't do that, miring me in another dilemma not of my design. I was falling for this alien, tumbling hard and fast. Huddled under animal hides in a cave on an alien planet cursed by an ice age, I'd never felt more treasured or protected. Torg had carried me through the snow, seen to my comfort, tended to my needs, and made me the center of his life in a few short hours.

Dakonians weren't the primitive people I'd expected but intelligent beings who'd suffered a huge setback in their technological evolution.

His sincerity, his honesty, his hotness made me wish I had come for romantic adventure and a chance for love, but unfinished legal business awaited me. Even if I'd intended to stay, the decision wasn't mine.

When the appeal came through, I would be summoned for retrial.

I forced myself to meet his gaze. "Escape." My answer fell short of a half-truth.

Heavy brows came together in a frown. "Escape from what?"

"I learned some things about certain people so I left."

"They were bad people?"

Bad didn't begin to describe the Carmichael organization. I eyed my wet clothing. Speaking about my former life even in carefully worded terms spurred an urge to grab my stuff and flee. "The worst."

"Darq heard a rumor that the females sent here had violated your planet's laws. Is that true?"

My stomach dropped to the cave floor. For a planet without electronic communication capability, gossip had spread fast. After I'd decided to be as honest with Torg as I could, he'd confronted me with this. Blood roared in my ears at the flood of possible consequences. Torg had ordered the banishment of a man for *attempted* murder. A court of law had *convicted* me.

If Torg exiled me, I would die in the wilderness. If, by some good fortune, I stumbled upon another clan

80

willing to shelter me before sending my ass to Terra, I'd still be doomed. It was too soon to go home. If I returned before my appeal reversed my conviction, I'd end up in prison.

I had to give Torg an answer. Outright denial would be foolish. The rumor was out there and would be confirmed by the other women who had far less to hide than I. Would they gossip about me? Whisper to their mates about the murderer among them?

If gossip did spread, confession now would enable me to explain on my terms. He *might* believe me. A rigged jury and a gullible public hadn't, but Torg might. Maybe. But if Torg never found out, it would be stupid to risk banishment. To risk or not to risk, that was the question.

In hindsight, we women had been too open about our crimes, laughing about them—or at least the others had. I hadn't. Mine was too serious. However, talking had been inevitable. As we'd gotten to know each other, friendships had formed, and we'd let our guards down. What else would you do on a three-month journey with strangers other than share the tie that united you? Still, I should have lied about my conviction, fabricated a lesser crime.

How would I tiptoe through this potentially

explosive situation?

"I heard that might be the case with some," I replied, controlling my tone and body language. My employment with the Carmichael organization had taught me to be a good liar. "But their crimes weren't serious."

His brows drew together. "But you left to escape bad people?"

Circling back to a question already asked was a common interrogation technique. I'd been "interviewed" enough to know. Torg didn't believe me. Or maybe he did and paranoia was taking hold.

"I worked for them." I skated the edge of the truth. First rule of telling a believable lie: stick as close to the facts as you could. "I needed a clean break to start over."

"I am happy to be your fresh start. Are you finished with your meal?"

The bowl rested in my hands, still half-full with my second helping. I'd lost my appetite. "Yes. Thank you."

He set the bowls aside. The fire had burned down to embers, and he tossed several logs on the coals. They ignited immediately. With a long stick, burnt at one end, he adjusted them. Fire seemed to need a lot of tending, unlike solar-powered heating. When the burning logs were positioned to his satisfaction, he rocked onto his haunches and rubbed one of his horns.

Were they bone? Cartilage? What other alien features might he have? Did he have a vestigial tail under his clothing? Was any part of his skin scaled?

He expelled his breath. "That thing you did—"

"Your horns—" I said at the same time.

We chuckled self-consciously, a moment of humor uniting us in ways I hadn't anticipated. Damn, I liked this alien. "What thing?" I asked.

"With your mouth."

Had I been making faces? I racked my brain for what I could have done with my mouth.

He pointed to his lips. "When I offered to find your friends…you brushed your mouth to mine. Is that how Terrans say thank you?"

"Sometimes." I shrugged. "Depends on the people involved and the situation. We have other ways, too."

"I rather liked that particular way." His husky voice drew my attention to his full lips before I lifted my gaze. Firelight flickered on his face, and a blush seeped over chiseled cheekbones. Good gods, he was handsome. "What do you call it?" he asked.

"Call it?"

"Mouth brushing. Is there a name for it?"

The translation should have popped into my head but I drew a blank. "You don't have a word for *kiss*?" I reverted to a Terran Universal word.

"Dakonians don't kiss," he replied.

"You're kidding?"

He shook his head.

"But you liked it."

He nodded slowly.

I leaned in until our breaths mingled. "Thank you for the dinner. And for keeping me safe out there."

His nostrils flared. Hesitantly, I touched his chest. His heart pounded against my palm. I closed my eyes and pressed my lips to his, letting them linger for a moment. When I pulled away, he groaned. My own heart hammered with anticipation as heat lit within. How far did I dare to take this? What would he expect? There were so many reasons not to pursue this. But, with my future uncertain, why shouldn't I grab a little comfort wherever I could find it? Selfish, but when I had tried to do the right thing, I'd ended up convicted of a crime. It could be years before I got off Dakon.

"I will have to find many reasons for you to thank me," he said huskily.

I smiled. "We kiss for more reasons than to say

thank you."

"For what other reasons do you kiss?"

"Sometimes…just because." I brushed my mouth against his again. On a hunch, I peeked at him. "You're supposed to close your eyes when you kiss," I murmured.

"Why?"

"Just because."

This time when I kissed him, I parted my lips and touched the seam of his. He jerked as if startled, but he opened his mouth and our tongues met in a tentative exploration. He tasted decadent, exotic, all male. I was relieved to discover that his tongue wasn't forked or anything, although the surface felt slightly rough, like a cat's. His touch sent shivers up my spine. He pulled me against his chest and kissed me with fervor. My alien charmer caught on quickly.

I cupped his face with my palm.

"Kissing is better with the eyes closed," he said.

We stared at each other, not awkwardly, but intimately. I drank in his dark heated gaze, the curve of his lips, the scruff of beard that had sent delicious tingles skipping along nerve endings, his horns. Curiosity was killing me. What did they feel like?

"Your horns…are they hard or soft?" I asked.

He dipped his head. "Find out for yourself."

I touched one. Warm. Leathery. Not as hard as bone but firmer than cartilage—and pulsing from the blood coursing through it. So, enervated tissue. Growing bolder, I ran my palm over the nub. It seemed to swell under my touch.

A growl erupted from his throat, a throaty masculine rumble so sexual, I jerked my hand away. Good gods, that sound. Pure sex. "Y-you didn't tell me…" My face flooded with embarrassment. Like a perv preying on unsuspecting passengers on a crowded airtrain, I'd groped a man.

"That's never happened before." He rubbed the horn and uttered not so much as a peep. "Try again." He grabbed my hand and brought it to his head. Maybe it was imagination, but the nub seemed to pulse more. I heard the start of a rumble, but he broke it off and sucked in a deep breath instead. I missed that growl. I *was* a perv.

"I'm sorry," he said.

"Why are you sorry?"

"The sound disturbs you."

In all the right ways, which, of course, made it all the wrong ways. This situation couldn't be allowed to follow its natural trajectory. Distance—we needed distance. I scrambled to my feet. My heart pinged in my chest. My underwear, if I'd been wearing any, would have been damp. Yeah, he had that sort of effect on me.

"No, it's my fault." Touching his horns had been a bad idea, even though he had invited it.

"How is it your fault?"

"I shouldn't have touched you."

"I liked it when you touched me."

My knees wobbled. "Y-you shouldn't say that."

He got to his feet. "Why not? I like you. You're my mate."

Those were the reasons! Touching him, getting that growly response gave me ideas I shouldn't be having, made me yearn for a real relationship with a man who cared about me. That epiphany shook me up. In a very short time, I'd begun thinking of a mating with an alien as a real relationship. I bit back a choke.

"Men on your planet don't have horns?" He changed the subject. Sort of.

"No."

"What do they have?"

My face surged with heat again. What was wrong with me? I wasn't a blusher. In my recent life, physical tells could have led to a fatality—mine. "The usual equipment," I mumbled.

"Like?"

I clapped a hand over my mouth and snorted through my fingers. Were we really having this conversation? "I'm sorry. I can't talk about penises with you."

A horrible thought leaped into my head. I'd assumed his bulge was his...but he was an alien. Who knew what he had inside his pants? "You do have one, don't you?" The question tripped out of my mouth. Maybe he had more than one...maybe Dakonians mated in ways we didn't. Just because they resembled humans didn't mean they shared the same plumbing, or that it functioned the same. Nobody on Terra had horns!

"Of course, I do."

"Just one?"

"I only need one. Would you like to see?" He cocked his head and smiled, a sly grin filled with so much devilish charm and so little remorse, lust careened on a collision course with good sense. Gods help me, I did want to see!

My face flamed.

Torg chuckled.

I ducked my head. Was he mocking me or flirting?

Or serious? The info vids hadn't discussed mating *habits*. Men here might woo their females by flashing. What had possessed me to kiss him? I felt out of my element. Not that I had an element. I'd had a few lovers, but men hadn't clamored to date me. Not on Terra or here. The other women of the *SS Australia* had been selected one by one until I remained alone. Then Torg had rushed in. He acted like he desired me now—but that disappointment when he'd first seen me had been real.

He tucked a finger under my chin. I expected amusement, but his gaze was serious. "Starconner, I am glad you came to Dakon. I apologize for my teasing."

"It's all right."

"It's not all right if I offended you."

"I'm not offended."

"Then what are you?"

"I don't know." I fluttered my hands. "Scared—but I'm not afraid of you." I dropped my gaze to my bare feet. Synthetic footwear had been inadequate. Terra One World had done little to prepare us, to prepare *me*. The others had volunteered, but I'd been shoved onto the ship with no forewarning or orientation.

"I was scared, too," he said quietly.

89

My gaze snapped to his face. "Why?"

"What if you didn't like me? What if you arrived and hated it? I had one shot to get a mate."

I did like him—too much, in fact. Nor did I hate Dakon. But I couldn't stay. His fears were as legitimate as mine. He had much to lose, too. I didn't want to hurt this man. It was unfair to lead him on, to sleep with him, to let him believe we were mates.

The earnest entreaty, the uncertainty in his eyes had the wrong words tripping from my mouth. "I do like you, Torg. The climate is a shock, but I don't hate it here."

His smile radiated relief. "I'm glad." Gently, he hugged me and rested his cheek against my head. His warmth enveloped me while his thudding heart drummed out a serenade. I was so done for.

I lifted my head to peer at him, and he kissed me.

Chapter Eight

Torg

I did that mouth brushing thing with Starr, and she melted against me, wrapping her slender arms around my neck. The sweet, exotic scent of her breath and taste stirred my desire. Before meeting her, I could not have imagined meshing mouths with another person, but I couldn't seem to get enough of it with her. Kissing her caused my manhood to ache with a fierce longing.

She felt so small in my arms. Dakonian females were much bigger, huskier. Almost as tall and strong as males, their quick swing could blacken a man's eye if he didn't duck fast enough. Starr didn't look big enough to hurt an insect. Her tiny stature, a concern at first, had become strangely appealing. I liked holding her, the way she fit in my arms.

I'd expected to desire coupling with my mate—that was part of the reason I'd wanted one—but the intensity surprised me. Flames of lust licked at my loins, set my blood to boiling.

Alien Mate

Until the Terrans' arrival, we had met no outsiders. If other clans had survived the apocalypse and lived on the opposite side of our world, we had no way to find out. The members of the fifteen clans were all the people we knew. Not all of us were friends, but none of us were strangers.

However, Starr and I were strangers, and I'd vowed to be patient.

One more kiss...

"I know it's too soon," I murmured against her lips. I'd awakened this morning alone. It seemed like a very long time ago to me. I wrenched my mouth away to bury my face against her neck, inhaling her alluring scent. Savoring it. Dakonians had a well-developed sense of smell, scent and taste merging into one. Would she think it strange that I sniffed her?

Do what's right. Be strong. "I don't want to push you into anything you're not ready for." My body protested, hating me.

"I'm ready."

Muscles tautened. The scent of her honeyed arousal worsened my hunger. I could almost taste her desire.

"Be sure." My voice was hoarse.

She lifted her hand and stroked one of my horns.

A shaft of rapture shot through my body. Even my fingertips buzzed. "I'm sure of you, and this moment." She rose up to do that kissing thing, but I was already there, plundering for more of her sweetness.

Starr clutched my shoulders with her tiny hands. When we broke apart for air, she went for the toggles of my tunic. She worked one loose in the same time it took me to undo the other four. I flung off my shirt, toed off my boots, and tore off my pants.

Starr's eyes widened with shock. Had I acted out of turn? Undressed too soon? I recalled her resistance to changing out of her wet clothing. Had I violated a Terran mating custom? The men there weren't that different from us, were they? Too late, I remembered her questions about my penis. I hadn't seen a naked Terran man—didn't care to—maybe all my assumptions were wrong.

A blush suffused Starr's neck and face. "Wow. You are...um...proportionate."

I dropped to my knees in front of her. "What does that mean, proportionate?"

Pink deepened to scarlet. "Well, you're a, uh, very tall man."

"I'm not so tall now. I'm sitting."

"Oh, no, you're still *tall*." She clapped a hand over

her mouth as laughter bubbled from her lips. I didn't get the sense she laughed *at* me, but I didn't understand her amusement, either. We had a lot of cultural differences to clear up—to be dealt with later. Eager to see her, I pinched the hem of the tunic she wore and tugged it upward.

Merriment ceased. Her eyes grew round as I peeled the garment off her.

I had no familiarity with the gods she often referred to, but their name sprang to my lips as I gazed upon her beauty for the very first time. Her smooth skin was free of blemish, unlike my own marked by scars incurred fighting beasts and hunting kel. Her bounteous breasts would fill my hands, the hard pink tips, my mouth. Her stomach pooched out with an alluring curve. And she was yellow all over. Well, not *all* over, but the nest of golden curls shielding the apex of her thighs was.

I hungered for her so much, I shook with the force of it. She was perfect. I don't know why the harsh words spilled out of my mouth. "You're too skinny." What a horrible thing to say! I cringed and braced for a biting retort and a cuff to the head. I deserved no less. "I-I...I'm sorry." An apology couldn't undo the hurtful words. Due to my loose tongue, my first mating would end in disaster.

She gaped. "You think I'm skinny?"

How could I repair what thoughtlessness had ruined? Her thinness didn't matter to me. Our women built up fat to protect them in our icy climate. Starr *was* skinny—by our standards. Some hearty kel stews and roasts would fatten her up, but if she never gained another pound, she would still be beautiful to me.

She flung herself at me, grabbing my neck and hugging hard. Her luscious breasts pressed against my chest; her curly mound brushed my manhood. She was so soft, so warm. I had to stay focused, try to fix the damage my impulsive words had caused.

She attacked my face with kisses. "That's the nicest thing anybody has ever said to me."

Nice? The translator had malfunctioned again, because she'd misunderstood. By a fortuitous error, I'd gotten a pass. Starr was sliding her naked body against mine and smashing her mouth to my lips. My horns swelled under her touch, sending sizzling sensations through my body. I groaned.

I stroked her unusual-colored hair, entranced by the liquidity of the long strands, which slipped through my fingers like water. *Slick as dog snot.* There was so much to discover. Her shoulders rounded softly over delicate bones. The indenture in her throat invited my lips. Her breasts filled my hands to overflowing. There, she was not skinny at all. I rubbed my thumbs over her nipples, and they hardened like illuvian pebbles but tasted as sweet as the berries we picked during the growing season.

As I suckled, Starr moaned and arched, her response heightening the desire already coursing through me. I needed to plunge my cock into my mate's body, but I needed to please her first.

I slid a hand to the yellow curls and toyed with them then delved between her legs. Conversations with other men who'd been mated had told me what to expect but hadn't prepared me for the revelation of her desire. Her womanhood had readied for me, releasing its honey to slicken her folds. An intense satisfaction, pride almost, swelled within me, exciting my cock to the point of pain.

When I found her pleasure nub and caressed with slow circles, her wetness increased, coating my fingers. Anticipation tightened in my chest as I probed her entrance and slid my finger inside. Slick, muscled walls squeezed. I could only imagine how it would feel to have her body grip my manhood. Soon, very soon, I would find out.

She nearly undid me when she wrapped her hands around my member and stroked me from base to tip, where my essence pearled. My cock had known no one's touch but my own. It preferred hers. My body shuddered, and I had to grit my teeth as lust burgeoned, surging so close to the surface I feared I would spill myself in her hands. I'd waited so long. I growled a warning, but instead of ceasing, she tightened her grasp around my manhood.

Before I shamed myself, I wrenched away. Later, when my control was not so tenuous, I could pleasure her slowly, multiple times. We had a lifetime of long nights ahead of us.

I flipped her onto her stomach and lifted her hips. She peered at me, her expression wry. "I should have guessed..."

"Guessed what?"

"Nothing." She tossed her head, flinging that beautiful straw hair over her shoulder. "We'll talk later."

"Talk. Later. Good."

Firelight danced on the moons of her bottom. Her womanhood glistened, desire scenting the air. I inhaled, filling my head and senses with her tantalizing essence. I guided my manhood to her entrance. The mere touch of wetness to my skin sent sharp excitement careening, but then an unexpected sudden doubt assailed me. My mate was so tiny. She'd been so tight around my finger.

I froze.

"Torg? What are you waiting for?" Starr lifted her hips higher and wiggled her bottom.

"I'm afraid I'll hurt you."

"You won't hurt me."

"You don't know that."

"Yes, I do. Trust me."

She believed what she said, but what if she was wrong? But when she wiggled again, hesitation caved. I grabbed her hips and thrust inside. Her womanhood hugged my cock, igniting a bliss so intense I saw stars. Saw my Starr. Currents of pleasure jolted every nerve ending.

Instinct took over my actions. Advance and retreat. A warrior's dance, a lover's entreaty. Sweat beaded on my forehead and stung my eyes. Muscles bunched. Rational thoughts did not exist anymore, save for one: *pleasure my mate*. I curled a hand over her hip to find her pleasure center. As I rocked, I stroked.

Starr moaned, and an answering growl rumbled

up from my chest. We were meant for this, she and I. My yellow-haired petite alien mate. Together, we moved in perfect sync.

Around my cock, her channel pulsed, and sensations spiraled through my manhood. Pressure and tension built at the base.

"Oh gods, I'm going to come," Starr gasped. "Oh fuck."

I did not need the translator to understand her cries of rapture. Having brought bliss to my female, I surrendered to my own. Pleasure exploded within me, and my essence spewed forth.

My knees shook as did the rest of my body, and I feared I could collapse and crush her, but I couldn't release her yet. Wrapping an arm around her stomach, I rolled to my side and tucked her into the curve of my body. Contentment and thankfulness filled me. For a moment, I couldn't speak, I could only feel. Union consummated, nothing would ever separate us.

Chapter Nine

Starr

"This is my mate!" Torg announced. "Her name is Starrconner. Please make her feel welcome."

"Hello, Starrconner! Welcome, Starrconner!" Greetings rumbled up from the crowd assembled a few steps below us.

Although two hundred people wasn't a huge gathering, it seemed bigger when everyone gawked at you like they'd seen, well, an alien.

Torg had called a meeting to introduce me to his clan. He'd carried in a pedestal of wood upon which I stood to raise my height closer to his so the people could see me better. They gathered in a clearing while Torg and I stood under the dubious shelter of a gazebo-like structure. Wind whipped in through the open sides to lash at my face. Still, the rest of me was quite toasty in my new kel attire: leather leggings and tunic, boots, the coat I'd been given the night before, and new mittens. I hardly noticed the smell.

A strong gust of wind tore the hood from my head,

sending my hair flying around my face. En masse, the crowd gasped. Eyes widened and whispers skittered through the assembly. What the hell? I gathered up my hair, shoved it under the hood, and glanced up at Torg. "What's wrong?" I whispered.

He managed to smile at me while scowling at the crowd. "They have not seen yellow hair before," he murmured.

"Oh." I eyed the Dakonians. There wasn't a single towhead among the sea of men with brown, almost black hair, dark eyes, and swarthy skin. I'd been taught staring was rude, but since they gawked at me, I felt at liberty to do the same.

They seemed huge to me, like furry bear-sized people. The women pretty much resembled the men in height, brawn, and fierce features. Only when comparing them side by side could I distinguish one gender from the other.

No wonder no one had chosen me. I looked like an alien to these people. Andrea, Tessa, and the other tall, dark women fit in better. I glanced up at Torg. He beamed with pride. I'd never seen a happier man. But would he have claimed me if he'd had a choice?

Don't obsess. Let that go.

A male stood in the front row, posture rigid, arms

folded. The hood of his kel concealed much of his face, but his bearing radiated disgruntlement. Torg had told me some men opposed the exchange program. Perhaps he was one of them. Or, in my nervousness, was I reading too much into it? I eyed the man. Uh no. Definite animosity. I sidled closer to Torg, and he slipped his arm around my waist.

"What is Terra like?" shouted a man in the crowd.

Torg raised his hands. "Starrconner arrived last evening. Please give her a chance to get acclimated."

"No, it's okay. I'd be happy to answer questions." He shrugged.

"Terra is much warmer in most places, and we don't get this much snow," I said. Not by a long shot. Here, snow weighted the branches and leaves of the tall trees, blanketed the ground, and piled in drifts against the caves. A hunch told me by the time the mild summer could melt it, winter would roll in with more. Probably some snow remained year-round. I supposed the polar regions resembled Dakon, but that was as close as it got.

"Most people live in tall buildings in large cities where there is little space. We move from place to place in solar-cell powered flying vehicles." I wasn't sure what they wanted to know.

"Do all females look like you?" another man called out. Side conversations ceased, and everyone stared.

Did he mean, were they all blonde, pale, and "skinny?" Were they seeking reassurance that they wouldn't be saddled with ugly women? I resisted the urge to touch my hair. Wasn't it my luck to land on a planet where my weight wasn't an issue, but my hair— previously my best feature—was? I couldn't catch a break. I glanced up at Torg. No, I had caught a break. A big hunky alien of a break. "More or less," I said. "I'm shorter than most women and fairer. Many Terrans have dark-brown hair, darker skin color."

The questioner nodded, satisfied with my answer. It broke the ice, and questions flew fast and furious. How long was the journey? What is a spaceship like? What is a flying vehicle like? How fast can it go? How many more women would be arriving?

"I don't know," I answered the last question honestly. Until I'd been shoved aboard the *SS Australia*, I hadn't been aware the program existed.

"Why did you come here?" demanded the scowling man up front in a feminine voice. He was a she!

Torg tensed. Why? Because of how I might answer, or because like me he sensed animosity? She couldn't possibly view me as a threat. She could have her choice of men. Okay, I had snagged the chief, the most eligible bachelor of the clan, but if she had wanted him, she probably could have had him before I'd arrived.

He's mine now, lady. So there!

Sheesh! I couldn't believe I was getting worked up over another woman's animosity—and I didn't even know if it was real or misperception.

Curiosity written on their faces, they waited for my answer.

"For a better life." I slipped my arm through Torg's. A better life—it could be true, if I didn't have to return to Terra. What did I have there anyway? If my conviction was overturned, it wouldn't fully clear my name. My case had been the trial of the century, and some people would always believe me guilty. I had no job, no close relatives who cared about me.

This could be a fresh start. I could do worse than an alien stud.

"You couldn't get that on Terra?" the woman persisted.

"That's enough," Torg said. "There will be more opportunities for questions later. My mate is fatigued from her long journey."

I wasn't the least bit tired. Wrapped in kel, curled

against Torg's muscular body beside the fire, I'd slept like a log. He was trying to protect me, and I appreciated it. What was her problem anyway?

The Dakonians started to shuffle away, but Torg raised his hand. "Wait. There is one more announcement."

They halted, and Torg's gaze flicked to the surly, masculine woman in the front. His expression hardened for an instant before he focused on the crowd. "By the law of the clan, I banished Armax this morning. He will not be permitted to return."

A few men nodded while surprise registered on other faces. "What did he do?" somebody asked.

"He attacked and gravely injured Yorgav."

Heads pivoted in the woman's direction.

"Icha remains with the clan as she has chosen Yorgav."

The notorious Icha! This sour woman had been the source of contention between the two men? Dakon *was* desperate for women if some chick built like a brick shithouse with a face and personality to match was worth fighting over. Even her name. *Icha*. Pretty darn close to Ick! I was being mean and catty. Especially since the hood obscured much of her features. There could be a raving beauty under all that fur—a beauty who I'd mistaken for a *man*.

Stop it! What the hell had gotten into me? Given that I'd been the last one chosen in the schoolyard pick, I had no room to talk.

But she'd started it with her scowls.

Take the high road, Starr. I inhaled a deep breath and allowed the icy air to cool my heated thoughts.

The crowd dispersed, and Icha sashayed away. If I'd seen the walk, I would not have mistaken her for a male.

"Thank you for indulging them," Torg said when we were alone. "I hope they didn't offend you."

"Not at all. I understand their curiosity." Everything about Dakon seemed strange to me, so it made sense my planet would be a mystery to them, too. "Yorgav will be okay, won't he?" Banishment had seemed extreme, but not if Yorgav's condition was as serious as it sounded. Torg pressed his lips into a grim line.

"Darq checked with the healer this morning. Yorgav's injuries are quite severe. He hasn't regained consciousness."

Dakon had no hospital. No medical school. What kind of training could the "healer" have? Maybe he was like a witch doctor, chanting and shaking a bouquet of feathers over the patient.

"I'm sorry," I said.

Torg gazed into the distance. "I am, too. We had a lot more, once."

"Before the asteroid."

He nodded. "We had hospitals. Buildings. Equipment. Schools. All of it is gone. Fortunately, a few healers survived, and they passed on their knowledge. The current generation can set broken bones, suture wounds, but they diagnose more than they can cure, and even that's difficult. We have no medicines, only herbal remedies." He made a wry face. "We can help someone with an upset stomach or a headache feel better, but those ailments aren't going to kill you."

"I'm surprised you only expelled Armax."

"Fault existed on both sides. Stealing another man's mate is a serious offense, so Yorgav is not blameless. Perhaps, I should have taken stronger measures, but it wasn't until this morning that Yorgav took a turn for the worse. I had separated the two men in the camp to defuse the situation. However, with Icha involved, problems would continue, so I opted for exile."

"Doesn't banishing Armax push the problem off

on someone else?"

"Most of our problems are interpersonal disagreements. Separating an individual from the person he has a problem with usually fixes the problem. Without Icha's influence, I don't believe Armax poses a danger to anyone else."

"But Icha will still be here, right?"

He nodded. "This is not the first fight she has caused. She often pits one man against another. She is supposedly quite skilled sexually and, before she chose Armax, she'd stirred much jealousy around the camp."

"So why not exile her?" I asked, and then answered my own question. "Because she is female."

Torg nodded. "We need all the females we can get, and when she is between mates, Icha shares her favors. The men would riot if I banished her."

"She has had more than one partner?"

"Many. She never stays with one man very long."

"But Yorgav might die."

"Yes. He might. "

I shivered at the grimness in his tone.

"My apologies!" Torg mistook the reason for my shudder and helped me off the booster. Literally and figuratively, he'd placed me on a pedestal.

What would happen if I fell off?

Dakon guarded their females, protected them, treasured them. Despite the trouble she caused, they kept Icha around. But they condemned violence. Would being female save me if they discovered I'd supposedly killed a man?

"Let's go to the cave where it's warm. It's time for our midday meal."

"Kel?"

"*Phea*." He grinned. "We do eat other food besides kel."

"Good to know." The stew Darq had prepared had been quite tasty, but I could foresee getting quite tired of kel, if that was all I ate. "Um, what's phea?"

"Fowl. Even more birds than animals died, but the phea survived. We eat the eggs, too. Unborn phea are quite a delicacy."

"Good gods, that's not what we're having, is it?" I'd take a chunk of kel any day.

Torg threw back his head and roared.

How wonderful that I could provide such amusement. I glared at him. He chuckled again and hugged me. "No, Starr. We will not have unborn phea." He picked me up and carried me toward his cave.

"Put me down, I can walk." I wiggled my feet to prove it.

"I like carrying you."

I buried my face against his shoulder. I liked it, too, more than I should, but I could worry about that later.

"It's all about survival for us, Starr." Torg tromped toward his cave. "We learned how precious life is, and every act is weighed to determine whether it enhances or detracts from our chance of survival. If I make the right decision, I live another day. If I make the wrong one, I perish."

Torg and I had something in common. That pretty much described my employment with the Carmichaels.

Chapter Ten

Torg

At the sound of a footfall, I sprang up in bed to find Darq entering the chamber. Starr slept beside me, one hand curled under her cheek, her face hidden by that mass of yellow hair. *Blonde*, she'd called it. It was growing on me. I liked having a mate who was unique, who looked like no one else.

"You have a visitor," Darq said.

"Who? The healer? Is it about Yorgav?" I whispered so I wouldn't wake Starr.

"No."

"Who, then?" I yanked on leggings and a tunic and shoved my feet into boots.

"Icha."

"What!" I forgot to whisper, and I checked on Starr. Still asleep.

"She brought a mating gift, insisted on handing it to you."

Since Starr's introduction to the tribe, members had been delivering kel hides, bone knives, pottery, baskets, beads, wood carvings, and enough food that Darq, Starr, and I could eat for a dozen planetary rotations.

"I told her to leave it with the rest, but she refused."

Typical Icha. She intended her gifts not to please the recipient but to shine upon herself. She demanded an inordinate amount of attention, and because she was female, she received it. I glanced at my sleeping mate. Thankfully, she wasn't spoiled like Icha. Though I had ached for a female to call mine, if Starr had never arrived, I would have spent my life in solitude before I would have accepted Icha. My mate gave a cute little snort in her sleep, and I smiled. Yorgav should be so lucky. He would have his hands full if he recovered. Would he think Icha had been worth all the trouble she'd caused him? Would cause him still?

"Any word on Yorgav?" I asked. "How is he doing?"

"Better. The healer says he shows improvement and thinks he might make it after all."

"That's good news."

Darq, the coward, left me to face Icha alone.

As I entered the main chamber, I found her eying the rack where Starr's clothing hung. They were dry now, but we hadn't removed them yet. The flimsy garments were near useless on Dakon, but Starr had insisted on keeping them. As Icha faced me, her expression shifted from assessing to coquettish. Nearly as tall as I, she managed to shrink several measures to appear smaller. She fluttered her eyelashes. "I hope I'm not interrupting."

I was quite certain she'd hoped for the opposite.

Icha had shed her outer kel to reveal clothing stretched taut across every ample curve. Cut low, the neckline of her tunic revealed the deep valley between her mountainous breasts. Men joked they could get lost in those mountains.

Her charms held no appeal for me. They never had, and now I had a mate who very much attracted me, who I would have been snuggling with if not for Icha.

"What is it?" I asked, barely covering my irritation.

She held out a covered basket. "I brought you some *macha* biscuits."

Macha was a syrup produced by a tree, on its way to extinction, making the syrup a precious commodity. The sap was our only sweetener, and we reserved its use for special occasions.

115

"You shouldn't have," I said. Icha gave nothing without expectation of reciprocity, but to refuse her gift would be an insult. Reluctantly I accepted the proffered basket.

She did not step away as she should have, but remained close. Our gazes locked. I was a hunter. I'd taken down kel many times my size, in addition to other more dangerous animals. I'd fought and defeated other men to win my seat as clan leader. I did not retreat from tough decisions. I survived in a cold, harsh land that killed without mercy.

Handling a predatory female was outside my ken. "Thank you. If that's all…" I moved toward the cave entrance, hoping she would take the hint.

She didn't.

I set her dubious gift on a table.

"I came to congratulate our clan leader on his good fortune and wish him well," she said in a breathy voice. If that was her real intention, then I was a spaceship pilot from Terra.

"The healer says Yorgav is doing better and might recover." I injected him into the conversation in hopes of warding her off.

"Good." She shrugged.

"You do not seem as relieved as one would

expect."

"Of course I am happy that an injured man, a member of our tribe will survive. Who wouldn't be? But if you are implying that I should have a deeper, more personal concern for his welfare…"

"Shouldn't you? You chose Yorgav over Armax."

"I did not. I merely wished to no longer be with Armax."

Anger surged at her manipulation and lack of remorse. "You'd better leave now." I took a few more steps closer to the entrance. If I had to, I'd pick her up and dump her outside. In a snowdrift.

Icha hesitated then picked up her kel and sashayed toward me. My tribe mates considered Icha to be the most attractive of our females. The sway of her hips, the purr of her voice drew men like insects to a weeping macha tree. I'd never trusted her, never desired to be one of a succession of men she used and discarded, so though she'd approached me in the past and my physical needs had been great, I'd rejected her. I was probably the only one in camp who had. As we had too few women, females like Icha would always have control over the male gender.

The coquettish look returned. "We could have been good, you and I."

If good meant disastrous. In my personal chamber, Starr slept, oblivious to Icha's visit. Thankfully.

"And we still can. It's not too late." She scraped her finger along my jaw.

I jerked away. "I'm mated now, Icha!"

"I can offer you so much more than the alien can."

The only thing she could offer me that I wanted was the sight of her backside as she left. "Not interested."

Her eyes turned flinty, but then she shrugged. "Your loss." She slipped into her kel and tucked the hood over her face. "Congratulations on your...mating," she said in a tone laden with condolence.

At last I got the view I wanted: her exiting the corridor. I headed back to my mate.

Starr was awakening. A tiny mound beneath the furs, she stretched. Her soft yellow hair contrasted against the darkness of the kel, stirring my manhood. "I guess I overslept." She sat up and tucked the furs beneath her armpits, shielding her body from my gaze.

My luck: the female I didn't care about, flaunted herself, and the one I wanted to see, covered up.

"I have a surprise," I said.

"What is it?"

"How'd you like to take a bath?"

Her eyes lit up. "Really? How?"

"Get dressed."

She frowned. "I have to get dressed to take a bath?"

"You can walk naked through the snow if you prefer, but we have to go to a different cave."

She scrambled out of the hides and into her clothes in record time. I enjoyed how her flesh jiggled as she rushed. Her breasts, while not as bounteous as Icha's, were large enough to fill my hands and then some. The memory of her softness stiffened my cock. I loved the wiggle in her walk, the way her buttocks shifted and her hips swayed in a dance all females seemed to know. But my female's performance was the only one I cared to watch.

"You're staring at me." She pulled on her boots.

I nodded. "Yes."

"I woke up, and you were gone."

"We had a visitor."

"Oh?"

"Icha," I answered, loath to mention her. Just invoking the name ushered in an ill wind. "She brought a mating gift."

She bent over her boots to lace them. "Was that all she wanted?" Her tone held an odd inflection.

"You don't like Icha."

"I didn't say that."

"I don't like her, either."

My mate's head shot up. "You don't?"

"No. She tries to cause trouble wherever she goes—"

Starr beamed a big smile.

"You find that amusing?" I asked.

"No. I'm just pleased you recognize she causes trouble."

"Of course, I see that. You'd have to be fool not to." Which meant the majority of my clan were fools.

Starr sauntered over to me. "Let's go take that bath, big guy." She clapped her hands on both sides of my head and planted a kiss against my mouth.

* * * *

Fresh snow had fallen overnight. The absence of tracks around the cave showed no one had been here yet today. Starr and I would be able to bathe in private. As clan leader, I could have shooed everyone from the pools, but I hesitated to employ special privileges very often because doing so invoked resentment among the tribe, as the previous leader had found out.

Males and females bathed in the mineral springs together with no concern for nudity. We had no more reservations about removing our tunic and leggings than we did in flinging off the hoods that covered our heads. However, Starr had explained that Terrans were modest and wore clothing as much to cover up their nakedness as for warmth. Revealing one's bare body to the wrong person or in the wrong moment embarrassed them. That my mate felt comfortable naked around me pleased me, and, strangely, her reluctance to disrobe in front of others gladdened me, too.

"You go first." I gestured. "The tunnel will be narrow, but it will descend to a large chamber where you'll be able to stand."

"Okay."

Doubled over with my head down, I followed her. Damp, warm air scented by minerals filled my nostrils. The baths were deep under the mountain, about a quarter tripta. Lamps burning an oil obtained from kel fat kept the passage lighted enough so that we didn't fall.

"I hear rushing," she said.

"We're almost there."

Moments later, we entered the main cavern, lit by

more oil lamps. Vapor clouds hovered over bubbling pools of heated mineral water. Mist condensed on the walls, running in rivulets into the pools.

Steamy air seeped into my bones and cleared my head. We didn't come here just to bathe; the pools rejuvenated us, or at least made us feel that way.

"Which pool should we use?" Starr asked.

"Can you swim?" I asked.

Starr bit her lip. "No."

"The middle one, then. The far one is quite deep; you would need to tread water."

"What about that one?" She pointed to the closest.

"That one is not as warm. You will like the middle one better."

Starr and I disrobed, and I wrapped our clothes in a kel hide and placed it on a rack to protect it from the mist. Everything in the chamber got damp. If we had to tromp back to our cave in wet garments, we'd catch a chill.

Naked, Starr padded toward the pool, her curves jiggling. For one so tiny and slender, her attributes were lush: generous buttocks, wide hips, full breasts. She was, to my appreciative eyes, perfect. To be called skinny was an insult, but my slip that one time had pleased her to no end. The intricacies of the female mind baffled me. Perhaps when we got more females and learned their ways, they would be easier to understand.

She stepped into the pool, waist deep for her.

"There's a ledge at the far end where you can sit," I suggested.

Starr waded in and submerged to her shoulders. She closed her eyes and leaned her head against the rocky edge. "Good gods, this feels so wonderful," she groaned. Her yellow hair floated on the water, frothing at her shoulders.

I joined her on the ledge. The shallow water lapped at my abdomen, barely covering the crown of my cock, which had grown rock-hard. It took very little provocation on her part to get me hard. I'd expected frequent relations to alleviate the rampaging lust; instead it had produced the opposite effect. The more we coupled, the more I wanted to. Even now, visions of pulling her atop my lap so she could ride me to sweet oblivion crowded into my mind.

She sighed, a pleasurable sound, almost like satiation. I was far from sated. We were still getting used to each other, figuring out each other's ways. I reached out and covered her hand. Her bones were so delicate, her hand so small, I engulfed it in my massive paw.

"This is nice. Thank you," she said, her eyes still closed. Lamplight bathed her face with a soft glow. She looked relaxed and serene. Oblivious to my need. We'd coupled twice during the night, but desire panted within me, hot and heavy. It never fully abated.

"So Icha brought you a mating gift," Starr said.

Well, that doused my desire by a measure.

"Us. She brought us a gift," I lied. Icha had intended her offering for me, and it was no gift. However, I knew better than to say so. I hadn't had a mate for very long, but that didn't mean I didn't have survival instincts.

Starr opened her eyes. "What did she bring?"

I released her hand and rubbed my neck. "Food."

"Have you heard how Yorgav is doing?"

"Actually, yes. The healer says he might recover," I replied, omitting any mention that Icha had lost interest in him and appeared to have set her sights on me.

"I'm glad." Starr stretched, arching so that the rosy tips of her breasts poked out of the water, and thoughts of Icha evaporated into the mist. My mate slipped off the ledge into the deeper center of the pool and submerged. When she reappeared, her yellow hair had darkened to a light brown. Water lapping at her breasts created the illusion the mounds bobbed on the surface.

Starr scrubbed at her scalp with the pads of her fingers then ducked under the water again. She stood up, and, with slow strokes, ran her hands along each arm from shoulder to wrist then moved to her breasts. Extra thorough, she palmed the undersides before rubbing circles around each mound. When she slipped her hands beneath the frothing water and widened her stance, a shaft of heat shot into my groin. I knew exactly where her hands were. Why hadn't I volunteered to help her wash?

Starr peered over her shoulder. "Would you do my back?"

I dove off the ledge with a splash. I thought I heard Starr giggle. I hauled her against my body. My manhood prodded her spine as I dragged my palms over her breasts.

"That's not my back," she chided, but wiggled so that her rounded buttocks teased my cock.

"You missed a spot." I pinched her nipples between my thumbs and forefingers then snaked a hand downward to cup her sex.

She gave a little moan. "What-what if somebody

comes in?"

I hoped that wouldn't happen, but it could. "Then, I'll kill them."

She giggled.

I explored her folds and found the little nub of her pleasure center. I'd learned a lot during our couplings: she preferred face-to-face, she liked long, slow strokes, and her wetness increased if I circled her clit before sliding my middle finger into her slick channel.

The beat of desire drummed. Blood pounded in my ears and throbbed in my cock. A primitive urge burgeoned within. Before I knew what I was doing, I bit her where her shoulder joined with her neck. Starr cried out but pressed harder against me and lolled her head, baring the delicate slope.

I licked the spot and tasted salt. Minerals in the water? Or blood? Remorse curled in the pit of my stomach, but it didn't prevent me from nibbling a path to her shoulder. Her skin was so soft. I slipped a second finger into her tight channel. She squeezed, and a shaft of lust shot straight to my groin.

"I need you so much," I growled against her ear. "Need you now."

I removed my fingers, lifted her, and prepared to thrust into her.

She wrestled away and pushed at my chest.

Dismay and shame twisted in me. One's mate needed to be wooed, not rushed. I knew that. Desire had overruled my good sense, my concern for her.

She planted her palms against my chest. "Sit on the ledge," she ordered, but the smile in her eyes, the glint confused me. I didn't know what to do—except obey—so I scooted to the pool's edge.

Starr closed her fist around my shaft. I gritted my teeth. She would kill me—or I would spill myself in her hand. Maybe both.

"I love how big you are. How smooth. How hard." She tightened her grip and pumped.

Her touch coupled with her purring words pushed me close to losing it. Fighting for control, I closed my eyes and sucked air through my teeth. "Y-you shouldn't say things like that."

"I love how your cock fills me up."

Was the translator not working? Or was this a test? Was she punishing me for my inattention to her needs?

Soft breasts brushed against my inner thighs as she moved between my legs. I opened my eyes. Her secretive, seductive grin was a kiss all by itself. Her thumb caressed the crown of my manhood, swirling in the essence that seeped out. Then she lowered her head and took my cock in her mouth.

Every nerve ending fired at once. Pleasure so intense I thought I would die snapped and curled inside me. I grabbed the edge of the pool and dug my fingers into the rock. "Starr...no...yes...yes...no."

Starr's body shook, and I knew she laughed at me. She laved my manhood, leaving no measure untouched. With her tongue, she traced the throbbing vein, circled the coronal ridge, and flicked at the weeping meatus. That was hard enough to bear, but when she sucked me so deep that I hit the back of her throat, my blood turned to molten streams of lava. I had never imagined such loving.

Pressure built, and I clenched my jaw and dug my fingers into the stone as if that could stop the tide.

She broke away, and short-circuited my strangled protest when she straddled my lap and impaled herself. Tight, wet walls closed around my manhood, gripping me in sublime rapture. When she rocked, control slipped from my grasp. I lost all volition. I grabbed her hips and thrust into her, racing toward the finish.

My ass scraped against the rough stones with every stroke. I grabbed the wet skein of her hair and twisted it around my fist, yanked her head back, and buried my face against her neck. I may have bitten her again. Need drove conscious thought from my brain.

Starr reached her own ecstasy, and her womanly core contracted, squeezing and milking my manhood. It surrendered to her, and I came, my body convulsing with rhythmic surges that wrung me out. Stars exploded behind my eyelids as I emptied myself into the brightest star of all, my mate.

Clasping her to my chest, I slid off the edge into the pool so she wouldn't get chilled. The minerals stung my ass cheeks, scraped from the stones, but I didn't care. For the moment, I felt replete. And guilty. I'd found my own rapture at the expense of my mate.

"I'm sorry," I said, when I could speak.

"For what?"

"For not tending to your pleasure."

My cock was embedded inside her, still partially tumescent. Her feminine core contracted around my member, and it responded with a throb. She craned her neck to stare into my eyes. That seductive smile curved her lips. "Are you kidding? I thought my body would break apart." She thumped my shoulder with her fist. "I had the best orgasm of my life. Couldn't you feel it?"

I nodded. Her contracting womanhood had triggered my release, but I should have been more attuned to her.

"When you bit me, something happened. I didn't think I went for that, but it triggered something in me. Fire shot from my neck to my pussy." She rubbed her neck.

I inspected the area. I had bitten her hard enough to break the skin. Twice, judging from the purpling wounds. I had marked her. I was appalled, yet deeply *satisfied*. She belonged to me.

Nobody will take her from me.

"You have a bruise. The kel will cover it so nobody will see," I said.

But I would know.

She was mine.

Chapter Eleven

Starr

"She's over here." Torg's voice floated in from far, far away. "You have to help her."

My guts were being twisted inside out. Sweat beaded on my forehead as I dry heaved into a clay pot. My empty stomach had nothing to expel, but the retching continued unabated. With a moan, I fell onto the bed of hides. I'd never felt so miserable in my entire life. My body shivered as if freezing, but I was burning up. Perspiration had soaked the kel beneath me.

The queasiness had begun last night before Torg and I had retired, but I'd managed to fall asleep. A couple of hours later, I'd awakened to dash for a clay pot and upchucked the evening meal.

Torg had wanted to summon the healer right away, but I forestalled it, certain the nausea would pass and uncertain what primitive medicine could do for me, anyway. I could live in a cave and wear animal hides, but subject myself to Stone Age medicine? Uh no. I'd let my immune system work out the problem.

But it was failing, and though the sun hadn't risen yet, Torg had overridden my protest and gone for the healer.

Torg and another man I surmised was their "doctor" knelt beside me. The healer frowned with concern, and Torg's expression appeared as stony as the cave walls, except for a muscle twitching in his cheek. His fists were clenched. "I'll be okay," I tried to reassure him.

The healer spoke. "My name is Stovak. Tell me what's going on." He set a kel pouch beside the bed.

"She's sick!" Torg said.

"Let her tell me." Stovak's eyes narrowed on my face. "Tell me exactly."

"I've been throwing up."

"How long? How often?"

"It started several hours ago. I felt a little queasy when I went bed."

"You didn't tell me that," Torg said.

"It wasn't that bad. I didn't think it was important."

Torg's eyes flashed. "Of course, it's important. You—"

Stovak held up his hand. "Torg, please. Let her

speak." He focused on me. "How many times have you vomited?"

"Seven or eight." I'd had two bouts in the time it had taken Torg to bring the healer.

Stovak glanced at Torg. "I need to examine her."

He made a disgusted sound. "That's why I summoned you."

"I must touch her."

The healer obviously knew my mate. He'd become a little possessive. He would not like another man touching me.

Torg's lips thinned, but he nodded. "Do what you need to do."

"Are you feverish or chilled?" Stovak placed his hand on my forehead.

"B-both." I shivered as a spasm shot through me.

The healer probed my neck with a firm but gentle touch. "No swelling, that's good." He placed his palm on my chest and tilted his head to the side. "Your heart is racing. Did that start when I came, or has it been doing that all along?"

Until he asked, I hadn't realized my heart had been racing, but he was right. "It started in the middle of the night, too."

Stovak removed his hand, sat back onto his

haunches, and frowned. "What have you eaten in the last day?"

"She had kel for the evening meal," Torg answered for me.

My stomach roiled at the mention of food and eating. I pressed a hand to my mouth and another to my stomach.

"Did you eat it, too?" the healer asked Torg.

"Yes. And Darq, also."

"How did you prepare it?"

"Roasted. With root vegetables."

I grabbed the pot and heaved into it. Nothing came up, except for a dribble of stomach acid that burned my mouth and nose.

"And earlier?"

"A mash," Torg said. A clan member had brought us a porridge of meat and grain."

Good gods, they were going to kill me. Every mention of food twisted my guts. "Stop," I pleaded.

"I'm sorry," Stovak said. "But I suspect something you ate is making you ill."

I flopped onto the bed. "Could I have some water?" My mouth tasted horrible. That alone was enough to make me sick.

The healer nodded, and Torg handed me a

tankard. I rose up onto my elbows, took a gulp, swished the water around then spat it out into the clay pot. The next gulp I swallowed, and my stomach reacted by churning. I pressed my lips together and squeezed my eyes shut. *Stay down. Stay down.*

"Darq and I have not experienced any ill effects," Torg said. "Everything we've eaten has been the same. "

Stovak asked, "This is true?"

"Yes," I replied. My stomach spasmed. "Except for the biscuits."

Stovak's eyebrows shot up. "Biscuits?"

"What biscuits?" Torg echoed.

"The ones over there. In the basket." I flung a hand toward the table piled with mating gifts.

Torg's expression turned so stormy, I gulped. "I thought...it would be okay...weren't they for eating?" It never occurred to me to ask permission. Had he been saving them for a special occasion? I'd assumed if the biscuits were a mating gift, they were for both of us, and I could eat them.

Torg shot to his feet and grabbed the basket from the table. "This is what you ate?"

"Yes."

He handed it to the healer, who took a biscuit and

sniffed it. "Macha." He took a nibble. His face hardened. "When did you eat this?"

"Yesterday. About mid-morning." I peered up at Torg. "You were out. I got a little hungry." I lifted a shoulder. "It didn't need cooking." On Terra, I'd been quite adept at using the flash-cooker which baked, boiled, or grilled food with a touch of a button, but managing a spit or a clay pot on coals from a wood fire exceeded my ability.

"You think macha sickened her?" Torg asked.

"Not the macha," Stovak replied, "but the *wheestile* added to it."

Torg frowned. "Wheestile isn't harmful."

"Not to *us*," Stovak said.

Good gods! Had I ingested an alien concoction poisonous to humans? The biscuits had tasted delicious, sweet but with a spicy kick. So good, I'd eaten two of them. My heart pounded with fear. "What's wheestile?"

"It's an herb we use for flavoring, but you have to build a tolerance to it or it causes upset: nausea, vomiting, chills, and sweats."

The symptoms I'd been experiencing. "Am I going to die?"

The healer's chuckle calmed my panic. "No. You'll

136

feel miserable for a while, but based on the onset of the symptoms, you've experienced the worst of it. I can give you a draught to counteract the residual effects."

Stovak handed the tankard of water to Torg. "Dump out most of this. Leave only a measure inside."

Torg's brows drew together in a fierce scowl. I'd never seen him so furious. He took the tankard, drained out the appropriate amount of water, and thrust it back to Stovak. From his bag, the healer withdrew a tiny pouch of crushed herbs and mixed a pinch into the liquid. "Drink this."

I clutched the cup and downed the contents. I expected my stomach to protest, but almost immediately, it calmed.

"Better?" Stovak asked.

"A lot, actually," I replied. "Thank you." Maybe the Dakonians had some science after all.

I was better, but Torg wasn't. He seemed to be breathing fire. "How many people are aware of wheestile's effects?" he asked.

The healer shrugged. "Not so many. There isn't a need to. We're all acclimated to its effects. A healer or a healer's assistant would know."

"Icha brought the biscuits," Torg said grimly.

Stovak's eyes widened.

"She would know, wouldn't she?" Torg asked.

"She never finished her healing apprenticeship," Stovak said, "but probably."

"Icha tried to poison me?" I gasped.

"I don't know about that…" The healer looked uncomfortable.

"I do." Torg's nostrils flared as he exhaled. "It surprised me when she delivered a mating gift; Icha is not a giving person."

Oh, she was a giving person all right. She'd given me a bout of vomiting like I'd never experienced in my entire life. That bitch. "What did I ever do to her?"

"You got the man she wanted," Darq said from the rear of the chamber. I hadn't realized he'd entered. "Icha isn't used to rejection." He moved closer. "How are you feeling?"

"Better now." My stomach had calmed, but my temper flared. I itched to punch Icha in the *macha*. Okay, she didn't like me—I hadn't much cared for her either, but I hadn't *poisoned* her. What kind of person did that?

Stovak repacked his bag and stood up. "She'll be fine. For the next day or so, have her eat light, drink lots of water—and avoid macha biscuits."

"Thank you for coming so quickly," Torg said.

"Please don't mention what occurred to anybody."

"I wouldn't think of it."

The healer left. Torg brushed the hair from my forehead and tucked the hides around me. "I'm sorry you suffered because of me."

I could get used to being cossetted. "It wasn't your fault. It was that she-witch."

Darq folded his arms and observed us. "What are you going to do?"

Torg sighed and stood up. "Since she came of age, Icha has incited discord. She has instigated countless fights. I haven't done anything because men choose their actions. They do not have to fight over her if they don't wish to. This time, she has gone too far. She deliberately hurt another person. *My mate.* I will not stand for it. Icha will be expelled from the clan."

Darq sucked in a breath. "There will be an uproar. When she is between mates, Icha shares her favors with many. The men will not appreciate losing her."

So she was a slut besides being a bitch. Perhaps I shouldn't be so catty, but the woman had poisoned me! Deliberately and with malice aforethought.

"What would you have me do? She tried to hurt Starr! If any man had done the same, we would expel him without hesitation or question."

"I'm not saying you shouldn't. In fact, I would do the same to protect my mate, if I had one. Just be aware of the possible reaction."

"Icha goes," Torg said decisively.

Warmth pervaded my entire body at the way he stood up for me. No one on Terra had done that. No one had spoken on my behalf. Not a single friend had visited me in prison. Nobody dared to mess with the Carmichaels. Maridelle had defended me, but, as my attorney, she'd received compensation and government protection to do it.

For a man to be willing to take on his entire tribe for me meant the world.

I could afford to be generous, to give Icha the benefit of the doubt. A frozen wasteland stretched between this camp and the next, and there was that tiny, tiny iota of doubt as to her culpability. I took a breath. "What if she didn't realize the wheestile would have noxious effects? The healer said it wasn't common knowledge. Maybe she did just bring us a basket of biscuits."

Both Torg and Darq shook their heads.

"She had enough healing training," Torg said.

"There are no coincidences when Icha is involved," Darq added.

I pulled the kel hide up to my chin. "It's freezing out there."

"She won't be in the cold for long," Torg said. "There isn't a single clan that wouldn't take her in."

"Because she's female?"

"Because she's female."

"Okay, then, you can banish her."

"I'm glad you won't be upset about it, but it's not your decision. It's mine." His face hardened, and I swear he thrust out his chest. His massive, muscled he-man chest. "After what she did, I would expel her whether you wanted me to or not."

I grinned. "I love it when you go all alpha."

Chapter Twelve

Torg

"How are you faring?" Enoki, council chief, fixed an assessing, speculative gaze on my mate. Perhaps I was being sensitive, but I did not appreciate the degree of interest in his expression or the level of solicitation in his tone.

"She's fine," I answered.

"Surely she can speak for herself."

"I'm fine," Starr answered.

"No problems adjusting?" Enoki asked.

Starr tucked yellow hair behind her ear. "No, everything is good."

Good, unless you took into account that she'd been poisoned by a jealous tribe member. Good, unless you noticed the angry glares male clan members fired at her as we'd walked across the camp this morning. I'd banished Icha two days ago. Even though I'd informed the camp of the reason, the friendship that had been forged when I'd introduced my mate had been undermined. Starr, an alien, served as an easy scapegoat. As long as Icha provided favors to the camp, they were willing to overlook almost anything.

"Glad to hear it," Enoki said.

He had no reason to doubt my honor. Did he think because I'd arrived late at the picking that I wouldn't treat my mate well? "Was that the reason for your visit? To inquire about Starr's welfare?"

We had convened in one of the smaller chambers of my cave. Enoki had been here long enough for a fire to burn down to coals and had yet to inform me of the reason for his visit. Was he checking up on me? Or was he interested in Starr?

"A week has passed since the females were paired with their mates. I thought it prudent to check on them. I am visiting all the camps. You're my first stop. I assumed you would like an update on the exchange program as well."

"Go on," I said.

"The Terrans were quite pleased with the illuvian ore and will double the next shipment of females. Since some tribes didn't receive *any* females in the lottery, the council has come up with a different plan. Each tribe will be allocated a certain number of chits based on size. Your tribe will receive two chits. It's up to you as chief to decide who to give them to."

"That's good news. The men will be pleased." Additional females would give them something positive to focus on. We would hold our own lottery for the chits; I wouldn't dare single out two men. How would I choose? It would be too difficult.

"Before they departed, the Terrans left us with computer and communication equipment, but we have no one who can set it up or operate it. They didn't have time to teach us," Enoki said. "They suggested some of the females might be able to help."

He looked at my mate. "Do you know how to operate the equipment?"

"I could figure it out." She nodded enthusiastically. "It can't be that much different from what I used on Terra. My friend Andrea Simmons would know how for sure. But I don't know where she is. She was chosen by a man named Groman. Maybe you could ask her, too?"

Enoki nodded. "I'll do that."

"And my friend Tessa Chartreuse. She went with Loka."

"I'll visit his camp today, as well."

"I'm positive with the three of us, we can get the equipment running."

"I had hoped you would say that. Perhaps we

145

could set a time, say one week from today, for the three of you to convene at the meeting place?" Enoki smiled at her.

Would he attend that meeting? I scowled.

Starr glanced at me then smiled at Enoki. "Perfect!"

"If you need anything at all, send word to me," the chief said.

If my mate needed something. I would provide it. A growl rumbled in my throat.

Enoki glanced at me, got the hint, and bade us farewell.

"What's your problem?" Starr jumped to her feet and glowered. "I'm going to the meeting place!"

"Yes. Next week."

"I want to see my friends. You told me I could when I first came. Besides, I need do something. I've worked all my adult life. I can't tan kel hide or cook over an open flame. Helping out with communications will give me something to do."

I lifted my hands and let them fall. "All good points."

"Then why are you mad?" she asked.

"I'm not mad."

"You scowled when Enoki asked if I could help."

"Not because you want to see your friends. It's normal to miss your own people."

"Then why?"

Feelings arose that I couldn't control, emotions I didn't want to admit. *Jealousy.* Icha had shifted her attentions from one man to another. What if Starr did the same? I was only the leader of a clan. Enoki headed all the clans and had far greater power and wealth. He could offer her more than I. I'd promised to find her friends, yet the opportunity to meet with them had come from him. "Because you smiled at him. He offered you something I couldn't."

Soft arms encircled my waist, and Starr pressed herself to my back. "Silly man." She didn't specify if she meant Enoki or me. "He can't give me what you can—a place in your arms."

"He has arms," I muttered.

"They're not yours. I only want you to hold me. Your body beside me." She rubbed her cheek against my back. "You protect me, care for me, cook for me, hold my hair when I upchuck after one of your females poisons me." She snorted.

"You laugh, but I failed to protect you."

"You stood up for me. You chose me over Icha. You banished her against the wishes of your tribe."

"It was an easy choice."

"And that's why I pick you."

I unfolded her arms and turned. "You would never leave me?"

"You would have to banish me before that would happen."

Chapter Thirteen

Starr

Fresh snow had pelted the ground overnight, drifting waist high. Torg led the way, taking short steps so I could follow in the depressions. Though I'd traveled this path once before, I recognized nothing. I never would have reached the meeting place without his guidance. Icha didn't deserve sympathy, but I still felt sorry for her, cast out into this frozen, harsh land. Torg had assured me she would be fine. Another tribe would welcome her, no questions asked.

He glanced back to check on me. I flashed him a thumbs-up, and he returned the gesture I'd taught him. It was spreading around camp. Other Dakonians had started using it.

"We're almost there!" he said.

"Wonderful!" He took good care of me. How quickly and firmly I'd come to accept him as my mate. I don't know if it was the way Torg had taken my side and stood up for me when Icha pulled her little stunt, or when he'd exposed his vulnerabilities after Enoki's visit, but I'd come to a decision: I would stay.

I must have been crazy to think of leaving anyway. Terra had nothing to offer me. Well, besides the climate. A woman could spend her entire life on Earth and not meet a man like Torg. He was strong, brave, caring, protective, and fantastic in the sack—or between the kel hides, as we liked to say here. I'd fallen in love with him.

If further inducement were required—which it wasn't—Dakon provided a haven from the Carmichaels. They couldn't reach me here. So what if a black mark remained against my name? I didn't live on Terra anymore. Here I was free, loved, and safe. Life was pretty damn good.

I would be reunited with my friends from the ship. I even had a job! I would help to get the computer system up and running. Then the next order of business would be to contact Maridelle and tell her to forget the appeal. I didn't want to waste her time. If the appeal came through, I would have to return for retrial, and I had no intention of doing that.

One possible glitch in present and future happiness would be if the Dakonians learned of my murder conviction since they frowned on homicide. Torg and I had bonded, so he probably wouldn't exile me, but I would hate to discover I was wrong. If my conviction became public, I would deny it and claim I'd embellished my criminal past to build "ship cred" with my fellow passengers. The Dakonians didn't have the means to check facts and disprove my story. They couldn't speak or read Universal Terran, and Andrea, Tessa, and I would be the only ones who knew how to use the communication system. My friends would keep my secret.

Torg and I tromped into the clearing where the meeting place was located. A dozen smaller structures formed a half ring around the big lodge. "There are other buildings!" I stared. Upon arrival, I'd charged head down, blindly following the woman in front of me. I hadn't seen anything but the stone lodge.

Torg stopped. "You thought the meeting place was only a building? It's the center of Dakon. The big building where we met is where the council convenes and we hold multi-clan meetings." He pointed to one of the smaller buildings. "The storehouse holds the bounty of the summer harvest. Next to it is a trading post. If we have an excess, we exchange it there for an item we don't have."

This was fascinating. I'd noticed next to nothing when I'd arrived. Beyond the structures lay a larger open field. I pointed. "Was that where the ship landed?"

Torg nodded. "I believe so. It had left by the time I arrived."

Typical of how Terra did things. The crew hadn't bothered to stick around to see how we were. We could consider ourselves lucky they'd landed the ship. They could have just slowed the craft, swooped in, and shoved us out the hatch.

I returned focus to the village itself. Torg and I stood at its edge. I pointed to a small stone building. "What's in there?"

"That's the records hall."

"Records? What kind of records?"

"Births. Deaths. Matings. While you are setting up the communication system, I will record our mating."

For my peace of mind, I would assume he meant mating as in alien-law marriage and not a notation of consummation. Let's have a little privacy here. Everyone assumed couples had sex, but we didn't need to announce it, did we? I drew my brows together. "Wait—you have a written language?"

"Of course we have a written language. How else would we keep records?"

His matter-of-fact tone held no hint of censure,

but my face heated at my prejudice. How else, indeed? Torg had explained Dakon had had a greater civilization; why assume they were illiterate?

"I'm sorry. What do you use to write with?"

"We mix ink out of ash and kel oil and hammer out paper from the fibrous stems of a plant. It takes a lot of work, so we don't waste paper or ink. When our infrastructure was destroyed, we feared we would lose our history as well, so survivors wrote down their memories. Those records are preserved in big tomes. That's how we know what happened."

"Could I learn to read Dakonian?"

"You want to learn our language?"

"I would like to know your history." The more time I spent with him, the more my admiration for him and his people grew.

"I will bring home some books and sheets of blank paper. Perhaps you would teach me your language as well?"

"I'd be happy to."

"Our children will speak both our languages and know both our cultures," he said softly.

My heart filled with happiness, but doubt nipped at me. Torg and I came from two different alien races. What if our genetics weren't compatible? Preliminary testing suggested they were, but it had yet to be proven. Nor would I put it past Terra to lie to get their hands on illuvian ore. I had seen my government in action. "I would like that, but what if we can't produce children?"

I knew for a fact they wouldn't come right away in my case. I had a contraceptive implant. Without the medical device to remove it, we would have to wait for the effects to wear off.

"We will still have each other."

The quiet simplicity of his comment brought tears to my eyes, and I blinked them away. "You make it so easy to love you." He was good and true and more than I deserved.

"I started to fall in love with you the moment I saw you."

A sweet sentiment, and his eyes radiated sincerity, but our meeting wasn't so long ago that I could forget his shock. I started to object, but he spoke again. "I learned then not to judge by appearance, but by deed and character. I love you, Starrconner, your yellow hair, your sacrifice in coming here, the way our bodies join in pleasure, your willingness to integrate into my culture."

He still often called me Starrconner. When I

taught him Universal Terran, I would teach him our naming structure. Or not. It was kind of charming how he blended both names as if they were one. I loved his gravelly, growly voice.

I hugged him hard. The bulkiness of our kels prevented my arms from reaching all the way around him, but he had no trouble and enveloped me in a tight embrace. Contentment and desire entwined. Torg squeezed me then set me away and jutted his chin at the lodge. "I think one of your friends has already arrived."

He was right. A set of footprints led inside.

"After I record our mating, I'll meet you in there."

"Okay." I kissed him. The frigid air had chilled his lips, but they warmed as we kissed. Torg headed toward the records hall, and I clopped through the snow toward the lodge. Who would it be? Andrea or Tessa? I couldn't wait to see both my friends. We'd bonded aboard the *SS Australia*, and though I'd committed myself to Torg, they represented my link to Terra. They had become family.

I flung back the flap and rushed inside. Hands on hips, a woman faced a bright, glowing computer screen set up in the corner. I recognized the braids. "Andrea!"

She spun around. "Starr!" Her face broke into a

huge smile, and we ran toward each other. We embraced in a clinging bear hug as if we'd been friends forever and had been separated for far longer than two weeks.

When we broke apart, we wiped at our eyes.

"How are you?" I asked. "How's Groman, your camp?"

"Good. It took some adjustment on my part. I'm still acclimating to the primitiveness." She swept an arm at the computer station. "I hadn't realized how hard it would be to be disconnected. Having this will help. I heard you recommended me. You're a lifesaver. Thank you." She hugged me again. "Tell me about your mate. I never got to see him. You had reservations. Are you any happier now?"

"More than I ever expected." It hadn't been my choice, but ending up here had been the best thing to happen to me. "My mate is Torg. He's chief of the clan I belong to." *The clan I belong to*. I would always be Terran, but, now, I was Dakonian, too. "Have you heard from Tessa?" I glanced around as if mentioning her name would cause her to materialize.

Andrea shook her head. "No. I can't wait to see her."

"How do you like Groman?"

Andrea made a sizzling sound like water dropping on a hot rock. "The guy is hot. He's built like a tank with muscles and lordy, what that man can do in bed." She grinned.

I blushed. The same could apply to Torg, but I wouldn't be so brazen as to say so. "The men appreciate us."

"And I love how they show their gratitude." Andrea laughed.

"How do the other women in the camp respond to you?" I asked, wondering if anyone had tried to poison her.

"They're friendly. Curious about Terra."

Lucky me. I was the only one with an icky Icha problem. Well, not anymore. Torg fixed that. "They really are desperate for women here."

"Yes, they are."

I moved toward the computer equipment. "You've set it up already," I said, relieved because I'd overestimated my abilities to Enoki so I could see my friends.

Andrea nodded. "Piece of cake. I want to check the delivery schedule. We can log on as Enoki. They gave him a code to use, which he passed on to me."

"I heard they're sending double the number of

women next time."

"I heard that, too. My tribe will get three chits next time."

"The Dakonians need women, but the population isn't that large. Torg's clan is two hundred-plus people."

"Groman's is around three hundred."

"Times, what, fifteen clans? They have maybe five thousand people, and they already have some women. What do you suppose will happen when they get all they need? They won't want an excess."

"No," Andrea agreed. "Terra will still need the ore, though."

"That's what worries me." Right now, relations were positive, but as I stared at the computer placed in a dirt-floored lodge, potential problems rose like the smoke spiraling from the fire pit. Had anyone considered future consequences? "When an advanced society encounters a more primitive one, things don't tend to work out for the latter." Earth history had proven that time and again. "Has anyone thought about that?"

"I doubt it," she said.

Earth's desire for the ore would become insatiable. Its population numbered in the hundreds of billions. If

Dakon got one woman for every man, its population might double to ten thousand. The shipment of ore had been small this time, but what would happen when demand increased? When they sent an entire fleet of starships?

"I can't imagine that Dakon will give the ore away without expecting anything in return."

"I wouldn't." Andrea shook her head.

"The council might decide to cut off the supply of ore. And even if they *didn't*, in the long run, it wouldn't work out to their benefit to have a technologically advanced civilization taking advantage."

"Terra could decide to take the ore by force."

"That's what I fear. We need to even the balance. Other than women, what does Terra have that Dakon needs?"

Andrea's mouth took on a wry twist as she glanced around the empty stone lodge heated by an open fire. "Everything."

I snapped my fingers. "Terra could help rebuild Dakon." A purposeful excitement curled in the pit of my stomach. They could have real houses with all the amenities like heaters, flash cookers, actual beds.

"Terra *could*, but will they? Right now, they're getting a two-for-one. They get rid of some 'problems'

159

and get free energy. They might resist paying with something of value. Dakon gives rocks they have no use for. The exchange program requires no sacrifice on anyone's part. Would Dakon even want the technology? It would change everything."

"Torg would," I said.

"Groman would, too, but from what I've overheard, a lot of men wouldn't."

"Then we show them what they're missing!"

Andrea nibbled her lip. "It will take a few years before Dakon has an optimal number of women. That gives us time to change the nature of trade, show Dakon what they could have, and better prepare them in case Terra ignores the treaty and attempts to take the ore by force. We need to get them up to speed fast."

"What do you propose?"

She cracked her knuckles. "First, we work on their defense."

"Weapons?"

She nodded. "If a battle was to ensue, as it stands now, Dakon would lose. A laser blaster will outgun a spear or a bow and arrow every time. So, we stockpile an arsenal. Laser rifles, fighter drones, defensive deflectors, surface-to-ship missile launchers. At the first sign of aggression, we'll blast them out of the sky."

Her face lit up.

She sounded more like an insurgent than a cyber hacker. She could have been smarter than me and lied about the charges against her. Too late to worry about that now.

"We can open a hospital. Order real medical equipment. Groman would love that."

"Why Groman?"

"He's a healer."

"You nabbed an alien doctor? Good catch, girl!" I slapped her arm.

She grinned. "This feels like Christmas. What else should we get?"

"Snow vehicles." I'd never forget that first hike when Torg had to carry me. "And portable comm units so tribes can talk to each other."

"Multipurpose drones," Andrea added to the list.

"Wait a minute...how is all this being powered?"

Andrea tilted her head toward the computer terminal. "Same way as that. Rechargeable solar cells. We'll need those, too."

"Does Dakon get enough sun for that?"

"Oh yeah. They can recharge from starlight if they have to. It would take a little longer, but it can be done."

"How are we going to get this stuff?"

"We're going to add items to the manifest. With every shipment of 'human capital,' they'll also receive weapons, medical equipment, and whatever else we want. Remember, I have Enoki's code."

"He has that kind of access?"

"Oh, hell no. His access is very limited. But that's all the entry I need. Our add-ons won't originate from the council chief—they'll come from the Terran exchange program director." She chortled and cracked her knuckles. "Mama is back in business!"

"You're going to hack in?"

"Does that bother you?"

"Not in the least. Our future is tied to Dakon's. The Terran government didn't have a whit of conscience about shipping us here." Who in this day and age traded people for rocks? That was called trafficking, wasn't it? Even if the women had agreed. Go to prison or go to Dakon. What a choice.

I hadn't even been offered that. My government had sold me out. No, I had no qualms about Andrea's plan. Hack away and sign me up to help. And get me a missile launcher while you're at it.

"Could you do me a favor?" I asked. "I need to contact my attorney and tell her to forget the appeal.

There's no sense moving forward with that."

"Sure, no problem."

I fidgeted, unsure how my next question would be received. "Um...did you talk to anybody about me?"

"I mentioned to Groman that I wanted to see you."

"Did you tell him what I was convicted of?"

Andrea shook her head. "No. I didn't tell them about any of us. They don't need to know Terra has been getting rid of their criminals."

Just because Andrea hadn't mentioned it, didn't mean no one else would. Among a ship of convicted felons, I'd been a *cause célèbre*. Not only had I supposedly killed somebody, I'd killed an infamous somebody. A Carmichael.

The exposure of my secret was inevitable, but I'd do my damnedest to delay it at least until the Dakonians got to know me better. Tessa and Andrea didn't have much to worry about. Tessa had laundered money. On a planet with no monetary system, her crime threatened no one. Neither did Andrea's hacking. On the contrary, her piracy was an asset.

I bit my lip. "I don't want word to get out about my conviction. Your computer hacking, Tessa's money laundering—"

"What about Tessa's money laundering?" a

cheerful voice cut in.

Andrea and I spun around. Tessa flung off the hood of her kel.

Squeals and hugs ensued.

"It's so good to see you." We were the three *amigas*. The two of them had drawn me out of my funk and isolation on the *SS Australia*, and I'd be forever grateful.

"I missed you guys." Tessa embraced me again. "I'm so glad we're all together again."

"I was beginning to think you weren't going to make it," Andrea said when we stopped hugging.

"Are you kidding? Wild kel couldn't keep me away," she said, and we laughed. "I was on my way out of the hut when Loka gave me that look...and we ended up dancing the horizontal tango. Dakonian men are a randy lot."

"And randy a lot," Andrea joked.

We laughed again.

"A woman on this planet could have her pick of men." Tessa snapped her fingers. "Hey, you! My hut. Don't be late." She giggled. "Anyway...so what's this about money laundering?"

"Only that your conviction and Andrea's probably wouldn't matter to the Dakonians. They don't have computers—or money, for that matter. My crime is different."

"You mean murdering your employer?" Tessa asked.

I winced. "Yeah, that."

"I won't say anything," she promised.

Andrea pantomimed zipping her lips.

"I didn't do it." They needed to know.

Tessa winked. "Of course not. None of us did. We're all innocent."

"It was self-defense."

I'd hit him, and he went down, but he was still alive when I fled the room. Jaxon had gotten to his feet and lunged for the weapon that had fallen from his pocket. He'd been bleeding, but head injuries always bled a lot, right? Honestly, I'd regretted not hitting him harder. I'd sprinted through the high-rise certain he would come after me, or that the guards in reception would detain me. I was amazed when I escaped. But not as stunned as when authorities arrested me the next day. If I hadn't defended myself, he would have shot and killed me.

"Sorry." Tessa hugged me. "I was just curious. I believe you. It must have been a horrible experience."

"It was." The government had set me up then

deserted me. I don't think they'd planned for the situation to go down the way it had, but they'd capitalized on it.

Fuck Terra. I hoped Andrea milked them dry. The more inventory she shipped here, the better. Weapons, medical equipment, vehicles, building materials— maybe some artificial snow-makers for the hell of it.

"Listen," I told Tessa. "Andrea and I think the rocks-for-brides program is destined for a short life span, so we're planning to squirrel away supplies and equipment to improve Dakon and make our lives easier. We'll have items sent with each shipment of women."

"That sounds like a good idea."

"We talked about medical supplies, transportation vehicles, solar cells, drones, wea—"

"Shampoo?" Tessa looked at Andrea hopefully. "I can't stand the smell of that stuff they make with kel fat." She wrinkled her nose. "And chocolate. And some synthetic fiber clothing they wear in the polar climates, so we can get rid of these kel hides."

I'd gotten used to the kel. I didn't notice the smell anymore.

"Sounds good." Andrea nodded.

"Snowshoes!" I added.

"We'll order a whole bunch of those." Andrea tapped her chin. "I'm wondering whether we should order a few items and build up to bigger shipments to avoid triggering an audit, or whether we should go for broke in case we get found out and they cut off the supply stream. What do you think?"

"A little at a time," I suggested.

"Go for broke!" Tessa punched the air.

"Maybe I'll skate down the middle."

I walked to the fire pit and tossed a couple of logs into the flames. "Let's get started!" I glanced at the door. "I expected Torg to be here by now."

"He's with Groman and Loka," Tessa said. "I saw them go into the tavern."

"They have a tavern?"

"Not by our standards, but it's as close to one as they get."

Andrea touched the computer screen. It awakened, and her fingers flew over the virtual keyboard. "Good thing we logged on now. The next ship departs in a week. The robos will have to hustle to load the cargo in time."

Tessa and I peered over her shoulder. In less than a minute, she'd accessed the shipment manifest and added a shit ton of stuff.

"How's that?" Andrea asked.

Tessa and I read through the list. "I can't think of anything else."

"This will go directly into the automated inventory system, which will scan the director's code then shoot the orders to warehousing so the robos can load the stuff onto the ship. Unless there's a spot audit and a live person familiar with the program reviews the manifest, it won't raise any questions. I also accessed the original Terra-Dakon contract and slightly changed the nature of the terms to include 'other needed supplies' to prevent any automated triggers."

"You're an evil genius," I said.

"Scary," Tessa agreed.

"Thank you." Andrea grinned. She sent the new orders with a touch to the screen. In a few short months, we'd be living in the lap of luxury. Relatively speaking.

"Anything else before I log off?" she asked.

"Remember, I want to contact Maridelle."

"Right. What do you want to say?"

"Tell her I appreciate everything she tried to do, but let the conviction ride. Tell her I'm happy, and I plan to stay here."

Andrea spun around in the chair. "Do you prefer a

textual communiqué....or would you like to talk face-to-face. I can activate the vid function."

Tessa moved to poke at a snapping log in the pit. Until we'd arrived here, I doubt any of us had ever seen an open flame, let alone tended one.

Maridelle might try to talk me out of my decision. She had fought hard, but I wasn't naïve enough to believe it had been for me. Like all attorneys, she desired to *win*. My conviction represented a loss. Of course she would push for an appeal. To take on the Carmichaels and triumph, well, that would be a huge feather in her cap—she could move from being a lowly public defender to a plum position in a criminal defense firm. Maybe I was being cynical. Or else I feared seeing any part of Terra again—even the inside of a public defender's office—would undermine my resolve to stay.

"Thanks, but the textual communiqué will do."

"Okay!" She fired off the message. "Anybody else you want to contact?"

"You could send a message to the Carmichaels to eat shit and die."

"Really?"

"No, but it's a nice thought." I grinned, feeling almost buoyant. Happiness, I realized. This was what happiness felt like.

A chilly breeze swept into the room as the flap opened, and Torg, Groman, and Loka stomped into the lodge, shaking fresh snow off their kels.

Dakonian men were handsome devils, but Torg was by far the most impressive. Groman was a tad taller; Loka had the most pronounced horns, but could not compare to Torg. Strength and honor were chiseled into the hard angles of his face, and his eyes glowed when they met mine. His grin curled my toes.

I ran over to him and linked my arm through his. Tessa and Andrea followed and stood by their mates.

"Torg, these are my friends, Andrea and Tessa."

I remembered Groman and Loka, but Andrea and Tessa made formal introductions.

"Do you have a lot more to do here?" Torg asked when we'd all gotten acquainted.

I glanced at Andrea. "I think we're finished?" She'd done all the "work." I'd assisted with the plot.

"For today." She nodded. "We can check in to track the progress of the ship."

"This is going to mean so much to our people," Torg said.

He had no idea—yet. I'd fill him in tonight. I wondered if Andrea and Tessa would tell their mates what we'd done. We should have discussed what to tell the men.

"Let me log off." Andrea returned to the computer system.

I hugged Torg's arm and then sniffed as an odd, yet familiar odor teased my nostrils. I squinted. "Have you been drinking?"

"I have imbibed a liquid, yes," he answered.

"I mean, alcohol. Fermented liquid."

"I had an ale at the tavern."

"What else does the tavern serve besides ale?" Was it like a pub? Could I order a kel sandwich to go with my beer?

"Just ale. Would you like one?"

I nodded. "I'd like to try it. Perhaps we could all go?" I glanced at my friends and their mates.

"I'm in," Andrea said.

"Me, too!" Tessa clapped her hands and gave a little bounce. I stifled a smile. Though eager to see it myself, I had a feeling the tavern didn't quite warrant that much enthusiasm. However, pleasure skittered through me. This would be a couples' night...er, afternoon. Three friends and their horned mates kicking back at an alien bar.

Tessa looked at Loka and then the other men.

"Maybe afterward you gentlemen would give us ladies a tour of the town?"

"Town" seemed like a rather grandiose description for the straggle of huts, but, again, I was eager to visit the "hall" of records, the trading post, everything. "I would love that," I said.

"For sure." Andrea nodded.

We women donned our kels and followed the men out. While we'd been in the lodge, enough new frozen precipitation had fallen to obliterate our arrival tracks, but fortunately it had stopped snowing.

As with the lodge, a heavy hide flap covered the doorway of the tavern. We pushed inside to a room scented by yeast. No jovial, loquacious bartender swabbed down the bar between drawing draughts of ale. A half-dozen corked jugs sat on a shelf. Tree stumps surrounded a couple of roughhewn tables. We were the only patrons.

And, come to think of it, other than us six, I hadn't noticed anyone else in the "town."

"Does no one come here? To the meeting place?" I asked.

"Only for assemblies, or if they need something, but each tribe is pretty self-sufficient." Torg tossed a log atop the embers in the pit.

He finished, and I smiled at him. "Buy me a drink, sailor?"

His brows knitted. "I don't understand."

Tessa giggled. "She means pour her an ale."

"How about a round for everyone?" Andrea asked.

"Oh! Of course." Torg plucked an earthen cup from a nesting stack. He poured out the dregs, and two thoughts struck me: one, small wonder the hut smelled so yeasty, and two, how many people had used that mug?

Andrea, Tessa, and I exchanged glances. Tessa looked horrified.

"The alcohol will kill anything." I shrugged.

"Even alien microbes?" she whispered. For a woman who'd run a prostitution operation, she was rather squeamish.

"Why not? It's alien alcohol."

"Besides." Andrea's mouth twitched. "There aren't that many people on Dakon. I doubt more than two or three thousand used that cup."

Torg eyed the tankard. "Is something wrong?"

"No. It's a Terran custom that we wash a cup before the next person uses it."

"But this one is not dirty. To replace the water used to wash it, a hole must be drilled into the ice to draw water—or ice must be melted."

No resource, not even water, could be taken for granted. Simple tasks took monumental efforts. These people needed our help more than they realized.

"Would you like a different cup?" He reached for another on the shelf.

"No, that one will be fine, thank you." The others wouldn't be any different.

I accepted the ale, and after Torg had passed a draught to everyone else, I raised my tankard high. Andrea and Tessa did the same.

The men exchanged befuddled looks.

"You, too, guys!" Tessa nudged Loka.

Hesitantly, they raised their cups.

"What should we toast to?" I asked. We had so many things to celebrate.

"To new friends and fresh starts!" Tessa said.

"Here, here!" I seconded.

The three of us touched cups. We motioned to our men, and they did the same. I took a drink. The foamy liquid pretty much tasted like beer until the afterburn kicked in. Pure firewater. I choked. Andrea gasped, too, but Tessa hadn't tasted hers yet.

"I've seen all I need to see." She giggled.

I took another exploratory swig. Once the heat

subsided, the ale wasn't all that bad.

The men pushed two tables together, and the six of us sat around and talked, swapping stories of our respective homelands. I was on an alien planet, but damn if this didn't seem normal. I never thought I'd say it—or be able to experience it—but my life was pretty damn good.

Chapter Fourteen

Torg

My mate staggered a bit as we left the tavern. I'd tried to warn her of the ale's potency, but she'd finished off her tankard. I blamed myself for her inebriated state; I shouldn't have poured so much. Dakonian females rarely touched the stuff. Groman, Loka, and I were all surprised when the females insisted on going to the tavern. Love-smitten males that we were, we'd indulged their unusual request.

Loka's female barely touched her ale, while Groman's held her liquor much better than my mate. Starr giggled and clung to my arm.

"Perhaps we should skip the tour," I suggested. We'd spent more time in the tavern than we should have. "We can do it another time." The sun had begun its descent toward the horizon.

"It will be dark soon," Loka agreed. Groman nodded.

"No, I want to see the rest of the...*town*," Starr said, and then burst into giggles.

I didn't understand what was funny about that.

"I want to see it, too." Tessa bobbed her head enthusiastically.

The other one, Andrea, nodded.

Groman and Loka shrugged. "All right," I conceded. "But we should be quick."

"Goody!" Tessa clapped her hands.

"We'll just peek in all the huts, promise," Starr said.

"All of them?"

"The hall of records first!" She staggered across the snow toward the building I'd pointed out earlier. Tessa ran up to her, and they linked arms. Andrea joined them. They giggled. We three men followed.

A cold, empty fire pit lay in the center of the records hut. We did not heat the hall of records because if the hut went up in flames, we would lose everything. Shelves bowed under the weight of hundreds of leather-bound tomes. Sheets of paper, wells of ink, and binding supplies were provided on a table for whoever needed them.

"Where's the book where you recorded our mating?" Starr asked.

"Here." I stepped to a book stand where the tome of vital statistics lay open so the ink could dry.

Starr peered at the book. "It doesn't look like hieroglyphics at all!"

"That's what I was expecting, too," Andrea replied. The two of them huddled around the book.

"It's a regular written language." My mate sounded surprised.

"Only not one I've ever seen," Andrea said. "It's nothing like Terran Universal or any of the dead languages. The symbols are completely different."

Their other friend, Tessa, took a peek, shrugged, and moved to Loka. He wrapped an arm around her waist.

"Is this our record?" Starr pointed to the latest entry, still wet.

"Yes."

"What does it say?"

"It has your name and mine and the date you arrived."

"Are we in the book?" Tessa asked.

"Yes," Loka said.

"We are, too," Groman added.

Starr ran a finger next to the list of recent entries. "Are these the matings with the Terran women?"

"Yes."

She nibbled her lip. "Your language

looks...challenging."

"Do you not wish to try to learn it?"

"No, I still want to." She rubbed the side of her head, behind her ear. "Too bad the implant doesn't instill reading ability, too."

"We'll start slow and easy." I moved to a shelf and searched among the titles for a few of the smaller books. I extracted two of them. "These will be good to start."

"What's so special about those?"

I pretended I didn't hear as I stowed them in my satchel and added some parchment.

"Torg? What kind of books are those?"

I shuffled my feet. She would be insulted, but she would need to start with something easy. "Children's books," I mumbled.

"You have children's books?"

"Not so many, because we don't have many children anymore, but a few, yes." The vocabulary in the children's books was simpler than in the others. I'd learned to read with these books myself.

Andrea hooted. "See the kel run. Run fast, kel, run fast."

Starr and Tessa laughed like it was the funniest thing they'd ever heard.

Groman, Loka, and I glanced at each other. We had much to learn about Terran humor. "The kel do run fast. That is why they are so difficult to hunt," I said. Aware of passing time, I asked, "What would you like to see next?"

"Trading post!" Tessa suggested.

"The storehouse," Starr added.

We stopped at the storehouse first where the females inspected baskets of grain, dried roots and berries, and the hanging slabs of dried kel. However, the trading post captured their interest the most. We did not discard anything; possessions were too precious. We might not need an item, but someone else might. An old boot with a hole in the sole could be refashioned into a child's boot or a carrying pouch. Tanning took a long time and a lot of work. Reusing materials saved labor and resources for something we *didn't* have.

The women chattered and touched everything: the kel hides, clothing, pottery, baskets, tools, and weapons. "I didn't realize how much I'd missed shopping until now." My mate held up a tunic with a beaded fringed hem. "This took a lot of work. Why would somebody get rid of this?"

"Perhaps they saw something they wanted more."

I didn't tell her the garment had belonged to a child who'd likely outgrown it. She bristled whenever her size was compared to that of a child.

"What do you think?" she asked her friends.

"It's cute. You should get it," Tessa said.

Her shoulders slumped. "I don't have a trade."

Andrea sidled up to her and murmured, "With what will be arriving in a couple of months, you could have everything in the trading post."

I didn't understand her cryptic comment, but if my mate liked the tunic, then she should have it. "You don't need a trade. I've brought items in the past and have not taken anything."

"So we have credit on account!" Starr said.

"I don't understand."

"Doesn't matter." She hugged the tunic to her chest. "I'll take it. What kind of items did you bring?"

"Hunting weapons." During the long nights, Darq and I often had sat in front of the fire and made bows, arrows, spears, and stone-bladed axes. If I hadn't been tribal chief, I would have been a bowyer or a fletcher. We already had several bow-and-arrow makers at camp, so I gave away most of my projects.

"Like this?" Andrea held up a bow-and-arrow set.

"Yes. That's one of mine." I'd dropped off four

artillery sets. I'd soaked wooden staves until pliable then shaped them into bows, using sinews from the legs of kel for the strings. I'd crafted arrows and quivers.

She examined it. "You carved the design on the limb?"

I nodded.

"Let me see!" Starr peered at it. "Those are animals! Are those kel?"

"Yes."

"So that's what they look like!"

Groman and Loka crowded around to peer at the bow. Tessa peeked, but then a basket caught her eye. However, the four of them examined the bow at great length, passing it among them and commenting.

Pride mixed with embarrassment to have my work subjected to such scrutiny. I crafted the bows merely to pass the time, but a little part of me lived in each one. "Your workmanship is excellent." Groman tested the bow's strength, pulling the string taut. "I would like to have this."

"You may take it."

Loka made a wry face. "I was just going to ask for it."

"There are others. I dropped off four sets." I

peered around the trading post. "But...they are not here. Someone has claimed them."

As a tribal chief, I mediated disputes. Angry, upset people brought me their problems to solve. A decision that pleased one man, upset another, so I received more complaints than praise. So, to discover others liked my work filled me with pride. The bow-and-arrow sets had gone fast! I'd dropped them off the day I'd come to claim my chit.

"I will bring you a set," I told Loka.

"I would be honored. Thank you," he replied.

"May I?" Andrea asked, and Groman handed her the bow. She held the grip, drew the string home, and released it. "Will you teach me how to use it? I would like to learn how to, er, shoot." To my eye, she looked adept already.

"I'd be happy to," he said. All males had at least a minimum proficiency with a bow and arrow so they could hunt for small game. Fathers taught their sons, and sometimes daughters, if they were interested.

"Do women here use bow and arrows?" Starr asked.

"Some do. Most don't because they rely on their mates to hunt," I said.

"You plan on doing some hunting?" Starr asked

her friend.

Andrea shook her head. "If I had to kill my own food, I'd have to become a vegetarian. But I figure it couldn't hurt to learn how to use the tools and weapons of our new home planet in case I have to defend myself."

"I cannot imagine that would be a necessity. Murder does not exist on Dakon. If it were to occur, it would be dealt with harshly."

The three women glanced at each other, then Starr studied the kel carvings on the bow.

"You have a word for murder, so you obviously know what it is," Andrea said.

"It existed in our past. Before the asteroid devastated our planet, we had a certain number of criminals. The catastrophe inspired us to appreciate life. To survive, we had to work together, to depend on one another. When we banded together, we bonded. Brother does not kill brother."

"Nobody has ever committed a murder since then?" Tessa asked. "What would happen if you did find a murderer?"

Starr must have thought her question impertinent because she scowled and motioned with her hand.

"No, there hasn't been a murder in centuries," I

said.

"Armax beat up Yorgav," Starr said. "And Icha tried to poison me. Those were violent acts—or at least acts of malice."

"And they were punished—exiled from the tribe." Had Yorgav died, no tribe would have taken in Armax after I'd banished him. Alone, he would have died in the wilderness.

"Icha!" Tessa glowered. "That horrible woman poisoned you? That's how she ended up in our camp?"

"Icha is in your tribe?" I asked.

Loka nodded. "Of course the chief accepted her. She is female. Icha did not say why she had been banished, only that she'd had a disagreement." He fidgeted, shifting from foot to foot, revealing something had happened, and if I had to guess, I'd say she'd attempted to seduce Loka.

"There are so many available men. Why does she make a play for the ones who have mates?" Tessa confirmed my hunch. She planted her hands on her hips and glowered. I'd bet Icha had met her match in this female.

I wiped a grin from my face. Loka had enough trouble without me laughing.

"An unattached man is no challenge," Starr said.

"Something easily acquired is not appreciated as much as something that is hard-won."

And that was precisely why we abhorred violence. Our survival had been hard-fought indeed.

"Let's not talk about Icha anymore." Starr glanced at her friends. "Are you ready to leave?"

They agreed. I rolled up Starr's garment and stowed it in my pack. Groman slung the bow and quiver over his shoulder, and we exited the trading post. The sun had sunk low upon the horizon. Even if we left now, by the time Starr and I reached camp, it would be dark.

"We should head back," Loka said. He could read the sky as easily as I.

"I know we need to go, but one more place, okay?" Tessa slipped her arm through his. Her smile hinted at mating favors if he complied. Loka's female had a little bit of Icha in her. Flirtation came naturally, and she used it to her advantage. There was nothing wrong with that as long as one didn't abuse the power as Icha did.

"One more. But, be quick." Loka caved.

As I would have if my mate had asked the same of me in the same way, but my practical, now-sober mate said, "I think Torg and I will head back to our camp.

It's a bit of a hike, and I don't relish doing it in the dark."

"Oh no! It won't be the same without you and Andrea. Come on, please? I promise I won't take long!"

Starr looked conflicted. I could tell she wanted to stay. "I would love to, but—"

"Moonrise will be bright this evening," I conceded. "We should have ample light to travel by if you want to stay a little longer."

Starr flashed me a smile that said Loka wouldn't be the only man to get lucky tonight.

"Andrea? Are you in?" Tessa asked.

She looked at Groman, and he nodded. "I'm in," she said.

"What's in the other huts?" Tessa asked.

"Those over there are emergency shelters." Loka pointed to the last two structures in the row. "Camps surround the meeting place at varying distances, so if you are traveling from one to another, you could spend the night here if you needed to."

"When the council of chiefs meets, sometimes the meetings run long, and some camps are many tripta away, so they board for the night, and go home in the morning."

"So the huts are like hotel rooms?" Andrea asked.

"I don't know that word," Groman said.

The three women glanced at each other. "Hotel," they said in unison, and laughed.

"I wonder if they rent rooms by the hour." Tessa winked at her two friends.

"There is no trade required. It is free to whoever needs it," I explained. "Do you want to see one of those?"

Tessa shook her head. "No, I know what a kel hide bed looks like."

"That leaves the hut next to the storehouse," Starr said. "What's that?"

"The apothecary," Groman answered.

"You have a pharmacy?"

"We have medicinal herbs available to anyone who might need them."

"Herbs helped me after Icha poisoned me," Starr said. "I'd like to see that."

"Me, too," Tessa said.

"Okay." Andrea shrugged, not as eager as the other two females. Since her mate was a healer, she'd probably seen a lot of jars filled with herbs.

Starr and Tessa skipped through the snow toward the apothecary. Like Andrea, I didn't find a bunch of earthen jars with dried plants interesting, but all this was new to my mate. With Groman and Andrea behind me, I tromped after Starr and Tessa. Loka trailed behind Groman.

Tessa kept up a steady distracting chatter. That female could talk! No wonder Loka hung back—he probably needed a breather. Once again, I thanked the fates that had delivered Starr to me.

Moonlight glinted on fresh snow.

Tessa slowed, turning around. "Hey, Loka—"

Starr proceeded toward the hut.

Ping! Whoosh!

"NO!" Acting on reflex, I dove forward and shoved Starr to the side.

My chest exploded with white-hot burning agony, and I fell.

Chapter Fifteen

Starr

My foot snagged on a root beneath the snow, and I kicked to free it.

"NO!" Something slammed into me, sending me sprawling into a drift. What the hell?

Andrea and Tessa screamed, and Groman?—Loka?—shouted.

I scrambled to my feet, wiping powder out of my eyes. I blinked. It didn't register what I was seeing.

Torg lay on his side in the snow, an arrow penetrating his torso as if he'd been skewered. Blood seeped through his kel to stain the snow red.

"Torg?" I still couldn't comprehend. "Torg! Oh gods, Torg!" I scrambled to his side. *Be alive. Be alive.*

He groaned and lifted his head, his pain-glazed eyes meeting mine. His mouth worked. "Are you all right?"

"Yes," I croaked. What had happened? How had he gotten shot? He needed help! Serious help. Like Terran medical facility help!

Groman and Loka raced over; the healer knelt. Tessa and Andrea crowded around. "Oh no! He's going to die!" Tessa echoed aloud my silent worst fear.

I couldn't stand to lose him. Where had the arrow come from? Had someone shot at a kel and missed?

"Nobody's going to die," Groman spoke in a calm tone, although I wasn't sure if he believed his own words. "Let me examine the injury."

What could a healer without medical facilities or any real equipment do? Herbs might settle an upset stomach, but they couldn't fix this! My body shook as I sucked back my tears. The red stain in the snow was spreading. Crying wouldn't help Torg. Instead, I grabbed his hand. He squeezed my fingers.

Groman undid the toggles and peeled back the coat. He exhaled through his mouth.

I bit my lip until I tasted the rusty saltiness of my own blood. "It's bad, isn't it?"

"No. It's better than I expected. The arrow missed his heart and lodged in his right shoulder." He shifted his gaze to Torg's white face. "He's not spitting up blood, so it didn't pierce a lung, either." Groman peered at Torg's back. "It went clean through to the other side, so that's good."

"How is that good?" I asked.

"Because the worst part has already happened. We won't need to force it through to remove it."

"You're going to pull it out here?" Tessa asked.

"Not here. For right now, the arrow itself is stemming the bleeding. When we withdraw it, he's going to bleed a lot, and we have to be ready to apply pressure. Let's move him to an emergency shelter. I'll work on him there." He jutted his chin at the apothecary. "I'm going to need some supplies. A painkiller, some antiseptic, and the coagulant."

"I'll get it!" Loka started toward the hut.

"No! Wait!" Torg tried to sit up.

"Hey, hey. Don't move." Groman placed a hand on his arm.

Torg gritted his teeth. "Loka…be careful…trip…wire." He took a deep breath.

Groman's brows drew together. "What are you saying?

"I think…someone…set…a trap." Even though it was cold, sweat beaded his forehead from the effort to speak. "I heard the arrow release."

I clapped a hand over my mouth in horror. "My foot did catch on something. I-I thought it was a root or a vine." A trip wire? A booby trap? So much for the Dakonian abhorrence of violence.

"I'll sweep the area before I enter," Loka said.

Torg nodded.

"Good. First, help me carry him to one of the emergency huts." Groman pointed to the trading post. "Somebody get me a large kel hide to use as a litter."

Torg started to protest, but Groman cut him off. "We've been in there already; it's safe."

"I'll get it." Loka sprinted for the trading post, retracing the path we'd followed to get here. Smart man. He wasn't taking any chances.

He returned with a large hide and a wooden staff.

"What's that for?" Andrea pointed to the pole.

"To check for trip wires."

Torg gritted his teeth and blanched when the two men lifted him. Andrea, Tessa, and I spread the hide on the snow then they lowered Torg onto the kel. Loka and Groman each took a corner by his head, Andrea and I grabbed the other two at his feet.

"Count of three," Groman said. "One, two, three."

We lifted. We tried to be gentle, but Torg groaned.

Trying to avoid jostling, we shuffled toward the hut. *I can do this. I must do this.* I held a corner on the lighter side, but Torg's weight threatened to rip my shoulders out of their sockets. Andrea didn't seem to be having any trouble, but she was bigger than me and stronger. Didn't matter. I had to muscle through. Torg had been shot with an arrow! *Buck up, Starr! Just do it.* The pep talk did little to provide the physical strength I needed. When I feared my arms would give out, Tessa grabbed my corner.

"Thank you," I said, tearfully.

"Everything will be okay," she whispered.

I rubbed my running nose against my shoulder. I couldn't release the hide or set Torg down because lifting him would jar him again. He'd nearly passed out from the pain the last time—although perhaps unconsciousness was preferable.

We neared the huts. "Let's set him down here for a moment," Loka said.

We were so close now, why stop? If *I* could make it, the men ought to be able to. "No, let's proceed."

"Better to take precautions than suffer the consequences. We should check for traps."

"Good idea," Groman agreed.

We lowered Torg to the ground. He bit back a groan, and I winced. Every movement hurt him, but better safe than sorry.

Loka grabbed the staff he'd placed on the litter. Approaching from the side, he swept the staff through snow in a direct line with the door. I held my breath, and maybe the others did the same, because an eerie quiet settled over the area. So quiet, this time I heard it. *Whoosh!*

An arrow whizzed through the air to disappear somewhere into the snow. If we had walked directly up to the hut, one of us might have been shot.

"Good gods," Andrea gasped.

Shock registered on everyone's face, especially Loka's. His jaw dropped. He hadn't expected to find anything.

With the staff, he pulled up a long vine. A bow sprang out of the snow near the door.

Groman pressed his lips together. "Keep sweeping. Make sure there aren't any more."

"Right."

With even greater care this time, Loka continued poking and prodding the snow, until he reached the hut and pronounced it clear. He returned to the litter; we picked up Torg and carried him inside. Gently, we laid him on a bed.

Groman lit a couple of oil lamps. Torg's lips were blue. I hoped it was from the cold and not blood loss. His bronzed skin tone had paled to pasty white. Little beads of frozen sweat dotted his forehead.

I hadn't been this scared waiting in the courtroom

for the verdict.

"I'll go get the supplies now. Anything else you need?" Loka asked.

Groman patted his pouch. "I have my knife, so that's good." He eyed the piles of fur upon which Torg rested. "See if you can grab some thinner hide for bandages. Be careful."

"I'll go with you," Tessa said. "I can get the bandages while you get the medicines."

Loka shook his head. "Stay here. It's not safe for you out there."

"It's not safe for you, either! What if something happened to you? I'm going! You can't stop me."

"Terran females are a lot like Dakonian ones. Stubborn." Loka glanced at the other men.

"I understood what you said!" Tessa glared at him.

"You were meant to," he replied.

Torg chuckled and then groaned. "Don't make me laugh. Please."

I hated to see him in any pain, but I was relieved he was alert enough to respond to the humor.

"Come on, then." Loka gestured. "Step where I step."

They left the hut.

Groman extracted his knife, and taking care not to

disturb the shaft, sawed off the arrow tip. "I'm not going to remove the shaft until Loka returns. Would you start a fire, please?" he asked Andrea.

"I'm on it!" Loka and Tessa were out retrieving what passed for medical supplies, Groman would doctor him, and Andrea was lighting a fire. I felt so helpless, standing there, clinging to Torg's hand.

Logs, kindling, and wood shavings had been stocked. Andrea knelt beside the cold fire pit, and with a piece of flint, ignited the kindling then fed the fire with larger pieces, until she had a blaze going.

"You're good at that!" Her proficiency impressed me. She was a woman of many talents.

Warming her hands over the fire, she peered up at me and shrugged. "I had to do something with my time. I learned how to light fires when Groman and I weren't lighting fires." She winked at him. A blush crept over his cheekbones.

The teasing intimacy speared me in the heart. That's what Torg and I had. What if he didn't survive? What would I do without him? Groman could remove the arrow, but what if Torg bled out? Or developed an infection later? The arrow had gone clear through the bone. What if he lived but the wound never healed properly and he couldn't use his arm, or he suffered pain for rest of his life? My brain found no shortage of dire possibilities. I swallowed my tears, determined to put on a brave face for his sake.

Torg wasn't fooled. He squeezed my hand. "I'm going to be okay." His reassurance made it even harder not to cry.

"Yes, you will." My voice quavered. I hoped my wish would come true.

A surge of cold air heralded Loka and Tessa's return. "We're back!"

Loka unloaded a pack of stuff: several corked earthenware containers and a big jug. "I got some water from the tavern. I figured you might need to mix a draught."

"Good thinking." Groman handed me his knife. He pointed to the hide Tessa held. "Cut some pads about this thick." He spread his fingers to the size he wanted. "Torg's wound will bleed, requiring several dressing changes, so we'll need quite a few, but get me a couple to start and then tear strips to tie around his chest to hold the pads in place."

Groman undid his kel and shrugged out of it, and I realized I'd begun to perspire. The hut had warmed considerably.

I removed my coat and set about performing my

assigned task, glad to have a productive way to help. The stone blade of the knife had been honed to a sharp edge on both sides. I gripped the hefty dagger by its wooden hilt and sliced through the leather. Worry weighed as heavy on my heart as the knife in my hand.

Groman sprinkled powder into a cup and mixed in some water. He helped Torg rise up on one elbow. "Here. Drink this."

"What is that?" I asked.

"A draught to dull the pain."

Torg emptied the cup. His mouth drooped. "That was awful."

"You'll be wishing you had more in a moment." Groman settled him back down. He dumped powdery contents from a different vial into another cup and added enough water to make a thick paste. He uncorked a jug, poured some of the liquid within over his hands, and rubbed them together. An alcohol smell permeated the hut.

"You can make alcohol?" I asked.

"You had some today in the tavern," he replied.

"You're using ale?" I didn't smell yeast.

"We further distill the ale and purify it for medicinal purposes." Groman shook his hands to dry them. "I'm going to remove the shaft then sterilize the wound, apply the coagulant, and then the pads. We'll need to apply pressure to stop the bleeding."

"Do you need my help?" Loka asked.

"No. I think Starr can help me. Why?"

"I have a hunch. I want to check on something." He moved toward the door.

Tessa followed him. "I'll come—"

"No." Loka's firmness brooked no argument. "This time, you stay here."

She crossed her arms and pressed her lips together. I wondered if they'd had a disagreement when they'd left the first time, but my sole consideration was for Torg.

Loka left, and Tessa joined Andrea by the fire. I moved to Torg's bedside. "How can I help?"

"Hand me the stuff as I need it." Groman grasped the arrow shaft and looked at Torg. "This is going to hurt."

"Do it," he said.

Groman planted a hand on Torg's chest. The healer's biceps bunched as he extracted the arrow. Torg didn't utter a sound, but he clenched his teeth so tight his jaw would probably ache in the morning.

Groman tossed the bloodied arrow shaft onto a table. "Help me remove his coat."

Together we eased Torg out of his kel. Blood darkened his tunic. We stripped that off him, too. "Hand me the antiseptic—the alcohol." I passed the jug.

He doused the wound.

My implant offered no translation for Torg's curses. I didn't need one. He jackknifed to a seated position, his hands balled into fists.

"Whoa." Groman stepped back.

"Sorry." Torg gritted his teeth.

"I still need to disinfect the exit wound."

Torg grabbed ahold of the kel hide. "Do it."

I pressed a knuckle to my mouth to keep from crying out myself.

Groman splashed alcohol over the back of his shoulder. This time Torg made not a sound, but sweat beaded on his forehead. Blood ran down his chest and back.

"Hand me the paste," the healer directed me. "And then two pads."

I passed him the mixture, and he smeared it into the wound. "This will help to stop the bleeding." Next, he applied a folded pad over the arrow's entry and motioned for me to do the back. Together, we applied pressure.

"How are you doing?" Groman eyed him.

"All right."

"Would you like another pain draught?"

"No." Typical man, he attempted to macho it out.

"Yes," I said.

"I don't need it." He shook his head, but I could tell that small movement pained him.

"Give him the pain draught." I overruled his stupidity.

Torg started to protest, but I cut him off. "Take it for me, okay? It hurts me to see you in pain."

"You don't play fair." Torg exhaled. "All right."

"Can you press on both sides?" Groman asked.

"Yes."

I maintained pressure on the wounds while Groman mixed up another pain potion and handed it to Torg who gulped it down. *Stubborn man. I know when I'm right.*

About the time the lines of pain eased from Torg's face, the pads had soaked through, but the bleeding had almost stopped. Groman maintained pressure while I retrieved two fresh pads, which we applied, and then he wrapped the long strips around Torg's torso and tied them into place. Next, he fashioned a sling for his right arm. "We must immobilize the limb to prevent it from pulling on the shoulder and reopening the healing wound." He stepped back and eyed his handiwork. "I think that will do."

Torg started to get up.

"Not so fast." Groman pushed against his good shoulder. "You shouldn't travel. You should spend the night. At the earliest, you might be able to travel in the morning."

"I must get to my camp; I'm tribal chief."

"Exactly. A tribal chief cannot afford to bleed to death."

"I'm fine now."

"We're staying," I said.

Torg's scowl revealed more acceptance than protest, for which I was grateful. What if he collapsed on the way home? What would I do? Torg could bleed to death out there. Without Groman's support, convincing Torg to remain would have been difficult. "Thank you."

He nodded. "If he remains still and quiet and allows the coagulant and his body's defenses to work, I think he'll be okay to travel in the morning. Andrea and I will stay in the other emergency hut. If he starts bleeding in the middle of the night, come wake me."

"I will. Thank you."

Loka entered with four bows slung over his shoulder. He struck the hut floor with his wooden staff. "I uncovered two other traps rigged with trip wires—one at the other emergency hut—the other at the trading post. How all of us managed to step over it, I'll never know. It was pure luck none of us triggered it."

"Good gods!" Tessa clapped a hand over her mouth. "One of us could have been killed."

One of us almost was. *Do you still think your people aren't violent?* If Torg wasn't injured, I'd shake him. He and the rest of his people needed to wake up and deal with reality. Armax had beaten Yorgav, Icha had poisoned me, and now this. How much more proof did they require?

Loka slipped the bows off his shoulder. "I collected the weapons for examination."

"Who would do such a thing?" Andrea asked.

"*Why* would they?" I countered. The why would tell us who. Had this been a random act of a sociopath who sought to hurt somebody and didn't care who? Or had an individual been targeted? Everyone I'd met had seemed very pleasant, except for...

Good gods...what if Icha was the perpetrator? Maybe I had been the target! Would she go that far?

205

She'd poisoned me, but the wheestile's toxicity wasn't fatal; if I'd been Dakonian, it wouldn't have bothered me at all. If she'd intended to do me in, wouldn't she have given me something deadly?

If it hadn't snowed, we might have been able to follow the tracks left by the assailant.

"We must notify Enoki and warn the others." Torg's face hardened like a Dakonian ready to kick some ass. If not for the dressing and the blood smeared on his bare torso, you wouldn't have realized he'd been severely injured.

"Perhaps this was an act, not of malice, but of poor judgment—someone unwisely placing a hunting trap," Groman suggested.

The man might know about healing, but he needed to wise up.

"No." Torg shook his head.

"No," Loka agreed. "Multiple traps were set to release when the person entered the huts."

"The perpetrator intended to inflict great harm," Torg said. "I'm sure your search was thorough, Loka, but in the light of day, we should repeat it to ensure all the traps have been found. We need more sweepers."

That's why *my* mate was a tribal chief. Even injured, he knew what to do and how to take charge.

206

And he knew a little something about people.

"My camp is the closest to the meeting place, a quarter tripta away," Loka offered. "Tessa and I will go back tonight. I'll talk to my chief, and we can return in the morning with additional helpers."

The closest camp, huh? Icha crept back into suspicion. She lived in Loka's camp. She could have sneaked out and booby-trapped the meeting place. My camp had been aware I planned to meet my friends from the ship. Everyone in Tessa's camp probably knew the same about her. So Icha would have known I would be here today. "How is Icha with a bow and arrow?" I asked.

"I see where you're going with this." Torg shook his head "Icha may be hotheaded and vengeful, but she is not a cold-blooded killer."

Hotheaded and vengeful sounded like motivation for killing to me! "She poisoned me."

"She made you sick. She didn't try to kill you."

"Maybe she tried but failed."

"I don't believe that, Starr. I would stake my life on it."

"You already have—and it almost killed you."

Torg held up his good hand. "Without more information, we can't settle this, and it's getting late.

Let's deal with this in the morning."

The lines of pain bracketing his mouth halted my protest. He needed to regain his strength and begin healing. We couldn't solve the problem tonight. In that, he was correct.

"Good idea," Groman said. "Remember, I'll be in the other hut." He looked at Loka. "You checked them, right?"

"I did. They're clear," he answered.

"If you need anything, come get me," Groman told me. "If he requires another pain draught, the powder is there. Mix a scoop with some water."

"I'll be fine," Torg said.

"I'll keep an eye on him," I promised.

"Tessa and I will leave now, too." Loka still had a hike ahead of him, albeit a shorter trek than Torg and I would have had.

The four of them donned their kels, and I hugged Andrea. "We're the next hut over if you need help," she said.

"Thanks."

Tessa and I embraced. "Be safe!" I worried about her tromping around in the snow. At least she didn't have far to go.

"You, too!" she replied, hugging me hard. "Stay in

the hut, and you'll be fine. Don't worry. We'll see you in the morning."

As they filed out, the fear that lurked in the background rushed to the forefront. Torg had almost been killed! I was defenseless on a primitive planet inhabited by dangerous people, present company excepted. The supplies Andrea and I had ordered couldn't arrive fast enough to suit me.

I turned toward Torg and pasted on a smile.

Chapter Sixteen

Torg

She tried to hide her fear, but my mate's smile wobbled. I held out my good arm. "Come here."

She moved to my bedside and gave me a loose hug. I tried to pull her onto the bed so I could comfort her properly, but she resisted. "You'll hurt yourself."

"I'm fine." It wasn't a complete lie. The agony in my shoulder had subsided to a dull throb. Whatever had been in the vile-tasting concoction Groman had forced on me had done the trick.

"You may not be in pain, but you're not fine. You're injured. You have to allow yourself time to heal." She pulled away. But she looked as forlorn as she was stubborn.

"Are you hungry?" I asked. Dinner wouldn't be grand, but the emergency huts were stocked with survival rations. We Dakonians were prepared— although we hadn't been ready for this little scenario. I couldn't imagine who could have set the trap or why. If I hadn't heard the *whoosh*...my blood ran cold. Starr would have been injured—or killed. I pushed the horrible thought from my mind. I'd go crazy obsessing about it. She was safe now. Morning would be soon enough to resume worrying.

"There should be some smoked kel." I pointed to some jars on a table against the wall.

Her stomach growled, and she smiled sheepishly. "I am a little hungry. I didn't realize we had food here." She tossed a log onto the fire then moved to the table, removed a jar lid, and sniffed. "Yep! Smoked kel."

She took out two large pieces and handed me one.

I patted the bed beside me.

She hesitated then scooted into place. Awareness of her nearness pulsated within me, and my cock stirred. Many hours had passed since our last coupling, but I had a hunch it would take coaxing to override her unneeded caution.

I took a bite of the smoked kel, and she did the same.

"Everything went well getting the communication system up and running?" I asked.

"Not a single glitch. Andrea and I added supplies to the next ship."

"What kind of supplies?"

"Medical equipment for one. And ground vehicles,

power packs, *weapons*..." Her face tightened, and I could tell she was recalling what had happened this evening.

I covered her hand. "We will find out who's responsible. It won't happen again. I promise you."

She shook her head. "It's not about that—although now I have another reason for wanting Terran weapons." Starr sighed. "Andrea, Tessa, and I were talking about the future. This whole illuvian-ore-for-mates arrangement sounds good now, but what happens when you have enough women?"

"We'll stop asking for them."

"I guessed that would be the reaction. Your needs may be filled, but Terra's appetite will grow. The existing treaty will whet their hunger for illuvian ore. They'll want more and more. They won't give it up. Will you let them take it for nothing?"

"Starr, it's worthless to us. They can have it. It's a bunch of rocks."

She slid out the bed, poured water from a large earthen jug into a smaller one, and placed it on the coals in the fire pit.

"What are you doing?"

"Heating some water for washing." She moved away from the fire and paced, swinging her arms.

"Those rocks are as important to Terra as females are to Dakon. More so because your need for women is finite. Earth's energy requirement is infinite. You have to be ready in case the situation gets ugly. I'm not saying it will, but the possibility exists. My people have been through this before, and it didn't end well. We decimated entire civilizations to acquire a shiny metal not good for anything except decoration. Illuvian ore can power spaceships and light cities. If you had harnessed its energy, you wouldn't be in the Stone Age anymore."

"But we don't have the means to harness it." The ore was valuable only if we could process it. Limited by wood bone, and stone tools, we didn't even have the ability to mine large quantities or put it to use if we had large quantities.

"My people are friendly and benign now, but you shouldn't be naïve." She punched the air with her small fist. "You have to shore up your defenses. At present, I think you have an advantage. The Terrans have superior weapons, but they have to travel a great distance to get here. Before they can invade to get more ore, they have to get more ore—which they don't have yet. Plus, you have climate on your side. You've learned how to deal with the severe cold; they haven't.

At the first sign of aggression, if you strike with a big show of force, they'll think twice."

Starr knew her people better than we did, and her vehemence made me think. What kind of people were the Terrans? The initial emissaries had been friendly and accommodating. The females were everything we'd hoped for—and more. I couldn't imagine a better mate than Starr. Her concern for our welfare confirmed her commitment to me and Dakon, not that I'd had any worries on that score.

Her warnings shouldn't be ignored. "I'll inform Enoki of your concerns."

"Thank you. That makes me feel better." She rubbed her hands together. "I'm not saying Terra would invade, only that you should stay alert. Don't take what they say at face value."

She removed the jug from the fire and tested the temperature. "Perfect."

"You're going to bathe?" I settled back, eager to watch. I never tired of looking at her. My horns and cock pulsed in anticipation.

She poured some water into a bowl and dampened one of the kel pads. "I'm going to wash you."

"Me?" I glanced down. Blood stained my torso. I grimaced. "I can wash myself. Give that to me."

"No, I'll do it." She ignored my outstretched hand and dabbed at my chest.

In the mineral pools, Starr and I bathed each other as a prelude to coupling, not because the other couldn't perform self-hygiene. I was no invalid. Would she spoon gruel into my mouth next? She would not respect me, would not see me as her protector if she had to play nursemaid. "I'm capable of doing that."

She ignored my protest, rinsed out the pad in the water, and resumed cleaning me. How humiliating.

I grabbed her wrist. "I will wash myself."

"I need to touch you, okay?" She glowered, but tears glinted in her eyes. "I almost lost you! Don't you realize how awful that would be?"

"I do know." I'd felt the same about her. I caressed the inside of her wrist with my thumb. I needed to touch her, too, and not in a casual way. I needed to be inside her, to hold her so tight and so close that nothing could slip between us, not even fear. "Why do you think I pushed you out of the way? I heard the bow release." Reflex and instinct had propelled me into action, but with remembrance, my blood chilled anew at how close I'd come to losing her.

It would take more than a shot from an arrow to kill me. But my Starr was tiny, delicate, fragile.

To soothe her, I would allow her to wash me. "You may continue, then." It came out sounding more imperious than I had intended.

Her mouth quirked. "Oh I can, can I?" She swiped gently at my chest. I'd succeeded in bringing a smile to her face, and that gladdened my heart.

"Why do you think the trap was set?" she asked quietly. "Was it a random attack, or was someone targeted?"

"I was the target." It was the only scenario that made sense.

"Why?"

"I've implemented unpopular decisions. Many people are angry with me."

"Over Icha."

"She's one reason, but also others objected to Armax's exile. Winning a chit generated a lot of resentment. Many assumed I'd used my influence as tribal chief to get one. Some men are jealous that I received a mate, while others opposed the exchange."

"If they targeted you, why set so many traps?"

"They couldn't be certain which hut I would enter."

She scrubbed at my skin with the rag, her touch no longer gentle. "So why set the traps at all. Why not hide in the woods and shoot you from there?"

I'd wondered that myself. "If he shot me directly, he stood a greater chance of being captured. Someone might have recognized him. Loka or Gorman would have chased after him."

"It's scary to imagine someone from our camp doing that." Her chest heaved with agitation, her nipples tenting her tunic. She sought a serious discussion, but I couldn't help but stare at her breasts as they moved beneath her clothing. Her womanly, exotic scent wafted up to tease my senses. Terrans and Dakonians smelled different. I could pick out my Starr from scent alone.

"That's only one possibility. The council of chiefs has five regular members, elected by the tribes. A sixth position is shared by the other tribal chiefs. As head of my tribe, I rotate with the others to share that seat. I'm outspoken, and I've convinced the chief to take some unpopular steps. I sat on the council when it decided to enter the treaty with Terra. I suggested the lottery— and won a chit.

"Some members of the other tribes claimed the selection process was rigged. Others opposed it altogether. I've made some enemies."

"If you made enemies as a rotating council

member, imagine how many Enoki has as the head of the council! Maybe he was the target."

"Enoki wasn't supposed to be at the meeting place today. I was."

"So were Groman and Loka! How could the perpetrator count on you being the one shot? It could have been any of us, or somebody else who happened to come today." She dropped the kel pad into the bowl of reddish-brown water and moved out of reach. "Maybe Groman's healing skills failed to save someone. Or Loka pissed somebody off." She paced.

"Those are possibilities, but I don't think so. Loka is very well-liked, and Groman is a gifted healer whose skills are in demand. People understand he can't cure everyone."

She asked good questions. Her reasoning couldn't be faulted, but answers couldn't be found tonight, and certainly not when other pressing needs had arisen. Heated discourse offered cold comfort.

I beckoned and shifted on the bed. "Um...could you help me..."

"What is it?" She flew to my side.

My ruse triggered some guilt but not enough to deter me. I closed my hand around her wrist and tugged. "Join me in bed." I flashed the beguiling smile that had softened her before.

"Are you crazy? You'll hurt yourself." She twisted her wrist, but I hung on.

"Then don't fight me." A hard yank, and she pitched across my lap. In a flash, I rolled her under me, ignoring the sharp twinges in my shoulder. I swooped in, but she averted her face, and my kiss fell on her ear. I teased the outer edges with my breath, and she shivered. My mate only pretended to be unmoved. I kissed her neck and heard the little moan she tried to stifle.

"You'll start bleeding again, and you'll have nobody to blame but yourself."

"Of course."

"The healer will demand an explanation."

Coupling came as naturally as eating or sleeping, and everyone who had a mate did it—a major reason why they desired one, but calling attention to our intimacies embarrassed Starr. "I will tell him to mind his own business." I used one of her idioms. Terrans had a colorful way of expressing themselves.

Arousal bloomed in her cheeks, and her thigh curled around mine, but she butted her head against my uninjured shoulder. "No, Torg. I mean it." She probably thought she'd looked fierce, but she had no idea how cute her little scowl was. She could glower at me all day, and it would only make me hard for her.

"Then we'll do it this way." I slid my good arm under her and rolled so that I lay on my back, and she straddled me. "You can do all the work," I said, but I lifted my hips to rub my erection against her womanhood. Through two layers of clothing—hers and mine—the heat of her sex warmed my cock.

"You're impossible."

"*You're* wearing too many clothes. Take this off." I tugged on her tunic and her leggings.

She sighed. Not the response I'd hoped for, but with a little persuasion maybe I could turn resignation into enthusiasm. I had to feel her against me, skin to skin, to imprint her touch, her taste, her smell. I had to reaffirm in a physical way that we were alive. One of us could have died today. I could not face the tragedy of losing my mate so soon after finding her.

Starr started to roll off me, but I grabbed her. "No, stay here."

She huffed. "Let me up so I can undress."

I couldn't argue with the logic, but I didn't trust her intentions. "All right." Reluctantly, I let her go.

She slid off the bed and smoothed her palms down her hips before waving a hand at the bed. "This isn't such a good idea…"

I knew it!

I rose up onto my good elbow. "Do you want me to jump out of bed and chase you, me being injured and all? Because I'll do it."

"That's—that's…not fair! That's like emotional…blackmail!"

"What's that saying you taught me? All's fair in love and war?" I flung off the kel blanket.

"Stop—all right." She flashed that cute little scowl and pulled her tunic over her head then wiggled out of her leggings. Luscious berry-tipped breasts bounced as she undressed.

I toed off my boots, but removing my own leggings—grown tighter by my erection—proved difficult with one hand.

"Let me help you," she said, not at all graciously, and tugged off my pants. My cock, hard and ready, sprang out, happy to be free, happy to meet her. Her breasts swayed, and I cupped one with my free hand, enjoying its hefty weight and how the beaded nipple poked my palm.

Two hands were better than one. I started to remove my arm from the sling I didn't need, but Starr stopped me. "No. You leave the sling on. If you want

this"—she drew invisible circles around her body—
"then you leave the sling on!"

I could live with those conditions. I stifled a
victorious grin. "Kiss me."

Starr crawled onto the bed and pressed her lips to
mine. We kissed tentatively at first, but then our
tongues met in a frantic dance that betrayed our
mutual fears. Her hair draped around my face, and her
heart thudded against my chest. Starr nipped at my lip.
"Don't scare me like that anymore," she murmured.

"No."

I tasted her, filling my senses with the essence of
my very own Starr. Like the lights in the sky, she
burned hot and bright for me. My irreplaceable mate.

At my nudging, she scooted upward. I captured a
nipple in my mouth. She moaned and clamped her legs
around one of mine, pressing her womanhood against
my thigh, coating my skin with the wetness of her
desire. My Starr might protest, but she wanted me,
too—and her objection originated from concern. How
could I lose?

I suckled one breast until the tip grew pebble hard
and red then treated its twin to the same. Starr
reached between our bodies to grasp my manhood.
Sizzling sensation shot into my belly as she pumped.

She pulled away from me then and shimmied down my body, teasing me by dragging her nipples over my skin. As she hovered over my cock, my essence beaded in anticipation. Starr smiled, and swiped at the liquid pearl with a fingertip then raised the digit to her mouth and licked it clean.

She lowered her head to trail her tongue from the ridge around my cockhead to my scrotum. With featherlight flickers, she teased my testicles before meandering to my cockhead, whereupon she circled the corona again.

Take me in your mouth. I thrust my hips upward. Hints were ignored, and teasing continued.

I twined my fingers in her hair. "Starr, suck me, dammit!" I stole one of her epithets to convey the seriousness of my need.

She gave a little snort of laughter and traced a leisurely trail to my manhood.

"Starr..." I gritted my teeth.

"Lie still and let me handle things. That was the deal."

"I don't remember making that deal."

"It was negotiated between 'you can do all the work' and 'all's fair in love and war.'"

I hated to have my own words thrown at me.

224

Disgruntlement evaporated when she engulfed my erection and drew me deep into her hot, wet mouth. Her lips closed tightly as she pulled on my cock. Nerves lit up like lightning flashing across a stormy sky as pleasure rained through my body.

I was at her mercy, but I always had been. The moment I spied my straw-haired alien mate, I'd been done for.

Employing her hands, her lips, tongue, and teeth, she pleasured me to the brink of ecstasy and, while I writhed, she pulled back to let the feeling subside then whipped my desires into a frenzy again. This time, I refused to be denied, and I grabbed her head, and thrust my cock deep into her mouth.

Muscles contracted as rapture pushed me over the brink, and I spilled myself with convulsive shudders, emptying and filling myself at the same time. Taut muscles went slack. Had I been on top, fucking her, I would have collapsed and landed on my injured shoulder. It would have been worth it, though.

Starr released my cock, licked her lips, and crawled upward to curl against my good side. I welcomed her into my embrace. She wedged her leg between mine, and her womanhood pressed against my thigh. Her sex was wet against my skin. I'd been selfish in taking my release; I'd done little to please her.

"I apologize for my selfishness. Give me a moment to recover and—"

She shook her head. "No, it's all right. You'll hurt yourself and start bleeding again."

Perhaps, but a man didn't claim his pleasure at the expense of his female. "I still want to join with you. I'll be careful." I would be dedicated and focused. I would make her scream with pleasure if it killed me.

"No."

Females could be very stubborn, but they rarely refused a pleasuring. It was their right and our duty. We protected them, cared for them, and pleasured them. Our needs came second. I had an alien mate, but I couldn't jettison everything I'd been raised to believe.

"What if I could pleasure you without hurting myself?" I asked.

She peered at me with narrowed eyes. "How?"

I nudged her. "Scoot up."

"What do you mean?"

"Just scoot up!"

Starr shifted and straddled my body. Momentarily distracted, I palmed a breast, stroking the nipple, before cupping her ass cheek with my good hand.

"Straddle my face," I ordered.

Her eyes widened.

"Come on!" I gave her ass a light slap.

She squealed.

"Do it." I slapped a little harder.

She complied and positioned herself so I had a perfect view of her luscious womanhood, its petals dewy with moisture, swollen with need. The scent of her desire raised my hunger again. Such sweetness, and mine, all mine. In this, I could indulge myself to my heart's desire and bring my mate to climax. How could it get any better?

I pressed on her thigh, and Starr obediently lowered herself to my mouth.

Chapter Seventeen

Starr

Bare to the waist, Torg had finished washing, and I had just donned my tunic when Groman and Andrea pushed through the flap. The next time we got on the computer, I would order some bells or solid doors to force people to announce themselves.

"How are you feeling?" Groman asked.

"On the mend." Torg winked at me. If Andrea and Groman had burst in ten minutes sooner, they would have discovered me riding Torg. So, yeah, he was fine. Healing fast for a man who'd been shot through the shoulder with an arrow. Either he had exceptional stamina and constitution, or natural evolution had come into play. The fittest had survived.

After licking me to the most stupendous orgasm of my life—twice—Torg slept through the night. I'd checked his injury once during the wee hours and found the bleeding had indeed stopped. When he'd awakened me this morning—horny again—he'd seduced me into intercourse.

While Groman examined him, a smirking Andrea sauntered over and whispered, "It smells like sex in here."

My face flamed. "Good gods! It does?"

She chuckled. "No. I wanted to see if you'd cop to copping a little."

"Now you sound like Tessa!" It was the sort of thing she would have said.

"The injury is healing nicely," Groman reported. "Don't do anything strenuous." He looked at me. "Clean it every now and then and apply fresh bandages."

I nodded. "Will do."

Stiff with dried blood, Torg's tunic was unwearable. He pulled his kel over his bare chest and did up the toggles. "Has Loka arrived yet?"

"Yes. He brought six men. They are combing the area."

"I'll go help them."

"No." Groman and I spoke in sync. Thank goodness I had someone on my side. Torg was incorrigible.

"Did you not understand what I meant by strenuous?" Groman scowled.

"That's not strenuous."

"To sweep through measures of snow with a staff will disturb your healing shoulder."

"Bah!"

"We have a long hike. Do you want me to worry the whole way home?" I dealt him a guilt card and didn't feel the slightest bit guilty for doing so. If the stubborn man wouldn't take care of himself, then I would have to do it. I regretted having caved to his seduction this morning.

He sighed. "What am I supposed to do, then?"

"Talk to Enoki," Groman suggested.

"He's here, too?"

The healer nodded. "Arrived with the others."

* * * *

Torg and I tromped through the forest. A forked tree with a notch in the trunk caught my eye. "I recognize that tree!" I snapped my fingers and grinned.

I tried to remain alert and pay attention to my surroundings, rather than training my gaze on Torg's back. Since I would live on Dakon for the rest of my life, I needed to learn the terrain. Subtleties emerged and stood out from the sameness: the forked tree, a thick fallen log, a stand of four precisely spaced conifers. I probably could find my way to the meeting place on my own.

Not that he would let me go alone.

Not that I wanted to.

I enjoyed his company and conversation, and I felt safer with him around. He'd heard the *whoosh* of the arrow releasing and pushed me out of the way. Any one of us could have been killed. Tessa or Andrea could have triggered the trip wire. Would their mates have been as fast in saving their lives as Torg had been in saving mine? He was powerful and fast, his stamina amazing. He acted like his injured shoulder didn't bother him at all.

Of course, Groman had tended him. He was obviously a gifted healer. Imagine what he could do when he got real medical supplies! Andrea, Tessa, and I had the power to make that happen. We could catapult Dakon out of the Stone Age, and, in time, restore them to their former glory. They weren't a primitive people, but an advanced civilization that had lost everything in a cataclysm.

Now they had a homegrown terrorist hell-bent on making things worse. On Terra, that type of person would have detonated timed explosives to eliminate whole groups. The only benefit to Dakon's primitive state was that their sociopaths didn't have the technology to wipe out a crowd.

Although he'd tried. Booby traps had been set at the apothecary, the trading post, and two emergency shelters. Fortunately, when Loka and his men had combed the entire compound, no more trip wires had been found.

"Why do you suppose the traps were set outside those specific locations?" I mused aloud. "Why not the tavern? The main meeting lodge?"

"Maybe they intended to set more traps but weren't able to finish."

"I think we were all targeted. He tried to hurt as many of us as he could."

"You might be right." Torg agreed, contradicting his previous assertion he'd been the focus. "Enoki believes the act is a protest against the exchange program, although he doesn't know if the perpetrator is angry because he wasn't chosen to receive a female, or if he opposes it in principle. The meeting place is where the females arrived. Maybe the perpetrator is making a statement. Some had argued against taking off-world mates on the grounds it would taint our bloodline."

So I was tainting a bloodline now? I took that personally.

"Most men recognized that while our genetic makeup would change, taking alien mates offered a chance of survival. Better to be half Dakonian than to cease to exist."

So Terran women ranked slightly better than death. Well, that made for a warm and fuzzy welcome. Torg didn't mean it that way, though. I knew that. The grins of the men when we'd entered the lodge after disembarking the ship had revealed how thrilled they were to see us.

And Torg was the best guy a girl could ever have. He took my hand. "I desire a mate to curl up in front of the fire with, to share my bed, to walk with me." He looked at me. "I am sorry this happened, and you were frightened. I promise, we'll find the perpetrator.

"Enoki has assigned a patrol to regularly inspect the compound for booby traps. He also has his master bowyer examining the weapons for clues. Each bow is as unique as the craftsman who created it. Though we all use a similar process, we can't help but leave our mark. It's like writing your name. The same people can write the same name, but their signatures differ."

"If you locate the man responsible, what then? What will happen to him?" Thus far, alien justice had amounted to kicking the perpetrator to the next camp down the path, although that hadn't been all that different from what Terra One World had done. They'd kicked a shipload of female felons to the next planet down the galaxy.

"The council will decide. New punishments will have to be established. Nothing like this has happened before."

"We women were supposed to be your solution, but we're causing trouble."

"You are the solution. Protestors will have to get used to the new Dakon. When they see the difference having mates makes in our lives, they'll come around. You and the other females brought us hope." He wrapped an arm around me and pressed a kiss to the side of my head. "*You*, Starconner, gave me a reason to live," he said, and then halted and stared off to the side.

"What is it?"

He pointed. Footprints came from the side and headed down our trail toward camp. "Somebody is visiting."

I eyed the depressions in the snow. "Two people."

We were almost home when Darq intercepted us. "I'm glad I caught you."

"What's wrong?" Torg asked.

235

Darq glanced at me then looked at Torg. "Icha arrived with a new mate. He's the chief of his tribe."

So Icha had mated up and bagged a tribal chief. Maybe now she'd leave me alone—or not. Like the proverbial bad penny, she'd shown up again.

Torg scowled. "Why is she here?"

"She has been visiting the camps with information."

"About the traps?" I asked. Word of mouth did travel fast.

Darq refused to meet my eyes and looked at Torg instead. "No, nothing about any traps. It's about the females...and Starr."

Torg glowered. "What about her?"

Darq's gaze touched on my nose then skittered away again. "Um, we should talk about this privately."

"I want to know what she said! I have a right." I glowered.

Torg nodded. "If it involves Starr, she should be told."

"She said Starr is a murderess."

My stomach plunged to my soles of my kel boots. I'd hoped I'd have more time, but there it was. What should I do? Lie and deny? Or come clean? Act shocked? Outraged? How solid was Torg's love? His abhorrence of violence was clear. Would he still support me if I admitted the truth? Could he forgive my conviction and my lies?

"That's preposterous!" Torg bit out. "Tell him, Starr—" My expression must have betrayed my thoughts. "Starr? It's not true, right?" His hopeful, pleading gaze almost unraveled me.

The truth would devastate him. But how could I lie to a man who deserved honesty? He cared for me. Icha was a notorious troublemaker. He would believe me because he *needed* to believe I wasn't a murderer.

There was no holding back the tide. If Icha went from camp to camp... I dug my fingernails into my palms and nodded. "It's...it's...true."

A silence so absolute descended on the wood, I could have heard a leaf fall.

"It's true?" He'd been shot with the arrow and hadn't been this stricken.

"I killed a man, but it wasn't murder. It was self-defense, only I got convicted. I was an informant for the government. They planted me inside an organized crime ring to get the evidence to convict the boss." Carmichael's tentacles burrowed deep into the judicial system. After my farce of a trial, I suspected Jaxon had guessed I was a plant from the beginning and gave me enough rope to hang myself.

I'd been placed to listen in and pass on conversations, movements, schedules. I'd discovered that Jaxon kept full records on a microdot. I'd already passed on a lot of information to the government, but they insisted on getting the microdot. It took months before an opportunity arose to search his office. One afternoon, I got a chance. Going item by item, centimeter by centimeter, I examined every speck on the walls, his desk, the windows. I found it underneath the granite service award he'd received for his contribution to an orphanage. I slipped the minute computer chip inside a tiny secret compartment of the necklace the government had given me and continued searching in case I found something else. That was my downfall. I must have triggered a hidden sensor because I turned around and there he was. I'd never heard him enter.

Jaxon said nothing, just stared at me, his eyes devoid of expression. Then there was the tiniest little flicker. His hand shot for his pocket. I grabbed the granite service award on his desk and swung it at him. He went down, and a laser revolver fell from his pocket and clattered to the floor. He scrambled for it. I ran.

To the outside world, Jaxon and his family had it

all: wealth, influence, and a community-minded spirit that got them lauded over and over. But they derived their real power from operations outside the law: drugs, extortion, human trafficking.

That orphanage Jaxon had contributed to? At least half the children were the offspring of mothers who'd disappeared after being kidnapped and sold into sexual slavery by Jaxon himself. He owned a brothel on a space station orbiting Mars. The Red Room served a clientele with more money than morals. The girls didn't work there by choice and had no chance of escape. That was one of the little tidbits I'd uncovered. What twisted pleasure had Jaxon derived in accepting an award for his service to the orphans he'd created?

I'd been a low-level civil servant key-tapper when the government had approached me. In the old days, they'd called us pencil-pushers. The organized crime unit had recruited me because—get this—I was a natural blonde without tattoos. Jaxon hired only fair-haired assistants, and he hated tats on women. The authorities created a new identity for me, gave me a makeover and a crash briefing, and sent me to interview with Jaxon. It was like going into Witness Protection without the protection.

Although Jaxon had been alive when I'd left him,

he later succumbed to the head trauma. I hadn't intended to kill him, and if I hadn't hit him, he would have killed me first. My government had sent me to work for a notorious, dangerous crime boss with no defense except my wits and reflexes.

As soon as I escaped the Carmichael building, I turned the microdot over to my government handlers. The next morning, I was arrested for homicide by a different branch of the same organization that had recruited me. I wasn't worried at first, certain the misunderstanding would be cleared up as soon as one department talked to the other department. Jaxon would have killed me! I was an informant, not a criminal!

Confidence turned to doubt then shock and horror as my case zoomed through the normally clogged and lethargic legal system like a case of judicial diarrhea: I was arraigned, indicted, tried, convicted, briefly incarcerated, and then exiled to Dakon. That I'd been an informant for the government had been ruled inadmissible in court. Jaxon's weapon had disappeared, although holographic vids obtained by the defense showed it skittering across the floor.

"I asked you about the rumor when you first came. You lied to me." Betrayal and accusation swirled in

Torg's gaze.

"I'm sorry. I was afraid to tell you."

"So Terra got rid of its criminals by shipping them here. What about the others?" Torg said through tight lips. "Are they murderers, too?"

"No. Their crimes were minor. Their participation was voluntary. They chose to come here. They wanted mates."

I wasn't aware of my slip until Torg stiffened. "They chose to come here, but you didn't?"

Was I masochistic or sadistic to confess such a thing? Torg knew the basic facts now; he didn't need to know how little I cared when I first arrived, that I hadn't planned to stay. It didn't matter how I got here or why I came, I loved him now.

"It's true I didn't have a choice like the others, but once I met you, I wanted to stay. You're my mate. Nothing can change that." I hoped nothing could change that.

He turned away. "You didn't want me."

"I do want you!" I grabbed his arm.

He shook me off like I was something dirty and stared over my head. "We need to get back to camp."

"Um, wait." Darq wiped a hand over his face. "There's something else you need to be aware of."

I braced for more bad news. Darq was a messenger of joy today.

"Icha has gotten the camp riled up, and they are demanding you banish Starr or step down as tribal chief. They're going to confront you."

My heart thudded. This was the last thing I needed. Would Torg banish me? I'd committed Dakon's ultimate taboo, and I'd lied to him. His tribe wanted me gone. He had every reason to exile me.

He cursed and stomped down the path. I ran after him and grabbed his arm again. "Please, Torg. Let me explain."

"Do not speak to me. I don't want to hear any more lies." He shook off my hold and took off. I had to trot to keep up.

"I'm not lying. I'm telling you the truth."

"Everything you said since you came here was a lie."

"No, it wasn't! I just didn't tell you the whole truth."

His scathing look cut to my heart.

"Can't you judge me on my behavior and not what I said?"

"I am judging your behavior. You murdered a man. And you lied to me." He stomped toward camp.

Yes, I had lied, and for that I was sorry. But while my actions had led to a man's death, I hadn't intended to kill him. I had struck him in self-defense—my life or his. Torg's refusal to give me a fair hearing twisted despair into anger. An eruption of red-hot fury burned through remorse.

I jumped in front of him, forcing him to stop. "What about *your* behavior? Huh? Mr. Holier Than Thou! I've done every damn thing I could to adjust to your Stone Age lifestyle, but do I get credit for that? Your life hasn't changed one iota since I came—but mine has gone downhill." That was true unless you counted that Torg nearly had been killed most likely because of the exchange program—and I was a free woman instead of a life-term prisoner, but those were quibbles, and I was pissed.

He tried to skirt around me, but I barricaded the path. "I remember your shock and disappointment when you came to redeem your chit! What right do you have to feel rejected? You didn't choose me, either. If I hadn't been the last woman left, if you'd had any other option, you wouldn't have picked me. If I'd told you at the start I'd been convicted of a serious crime, you would have forfeited your chit. You would have gone without a female rather than take me."

He reddened, confirming my read of his initial reaction, and it further fueled my anger and hurt. "And don't you dare lecture to me about criminals! Armax damn near beat Yorgav to death. Icha poisoned me, and now you have some sociopath terrorist serial killer running around booby trapping that makeshift excuse for a town." I jabbed his chest with my finger but avoided his injury. "You're not perfect!" Poke. "Your people and your fucking frozen wasteland of a planet aren't perfect." Jab. "And you have no fucking idea what the hell I've been through." I jabbed him extra hard then ran for the camp so he wouldn't see me cry.

Chapter Eighteen

Torg

Shame scalded my throat. I'd hurt Starr terribly, and suddenly the pain she'd caused me didn't matter anymore. I was horrified that she had known of my shock when I'd first laid eyes on her. She was beautiful to me now, and I loved her to the depths of my being. That's why I'd felt so betrayed by her lies.

If I expected honesty from her, shouldn't I demand the same from myself? If she had told me the truth in the beginning, I would have rejected her. Just like she guessed.

But now I loved her, and I *knew* her. If Starr said the killing was self-defense, then I believed her because I did judge by behavior, and everything Starr had done since she'd arrived revealed what kind of person she was. My Starr was good and kind.

I had to apologize and mend the rift. I started after her, but Darq grabbed my arm.

"Let her go. When females get angry, the best you can do is stay out of the way until they cool down. I suspect Terran ones aren't much different."

"She's not just angry, she's hurt."

"Which you can't fix in the time you have available." Darq's expression was worried. "The situation is serious. They are talking about expelling *you* from the tribe whether or not you banish Starr. They're furious you exiled Icha because of Starr who is a murderess—or not," he amended after glancing at my face. "I'm only telling you what they're saying."

Starr was about to disappear around the bend. We weren't more than a quarter tripta from camp. "All the more reason to go after her. I don't want her to march into camp with everyone in an uproar."

He nodded. "She would rile them further, and there's no telling what state they'll be in. Icha was whipping them up into a frenzy when I left. You have to deal with them now. I'll intercept Starr and escort her to the cave. We'll circle around to the rear so no one sees."

I sighed. That was the best solution, but I didn't like it. Sometimes I hated being tribal chief. "All right," I agreed. "Tell Starr I'm sorry."

"I doubt she'll listen to me. Tell her yourself when you see her. I'll keep her safe." Darq jogged after my mate.

* * * *

"Not fit to be chief!"

"He should be banished—and the Terran, too!"

"Criminals, all of them."

Angry voices filtered through the trees. Darq hadn't exaggerated the rancor, and I was grateful for the warning and for him taking care of Starr when I couldn't. A deep breath shored up my fortitude, and then I strode into the clearing where I'd introduced her to everyone. If anyone from the tribe was missing, you couldn't tell. It appeared as though every male and female had gathered. They faced the dais upon which Icha and her new mate stood.

"Terra is sending their criminals to our planet!" Icha shouted. "Are those the kind of females you desire? A murderess who might kill you in your sleep?"

Her mate nudged her, and Icha spotted me. "There he is!" she shouted.

Half the people scowled at me, while others avoided my gaze like naughty children caught misbehaving. I pushed my way through the crowd and stomped onto the dais, forcing Icha and Frokel to make room for me. I'd met Frokel at council meetings. I hadn't liked him then, and the present situation didn't improve my estimation. "What is the meaning of this?" I demanded.

Before either of them could answer, someone shouted from the crowd. "Is it true? Are the females murderers?"

At least someone had the sense to ask, but unfortunately, the answer would not have a positive effect. How I wished Starr had confessed sooner so I had time to prepare, to meet with the others who had Terran mates and come up with a plan.

Icha smirked with triumph. Terra had sent *us* the women they didn't want. If the exchange program had allowed a reciprocal arrangement, I'd personally escort Icha to the first ship to Earth.

My tribe stared at me, waiting for a response. Words had to be chosen carefully. "I recently learned the women who volunteered to come to Dakon had broken Terran laws."

"Sounds like criminals to me!" someone yelled, and a cacophony of agreement buzzed through the crowd.

At the edge, I spied Darq. Why had he left Starr alone? What if she ventured out? Her presence would be like dumping kel oil on an open flame. Unable to signal him without drawing attention, I could only hope he'd return to the cave soon. I wished I was there.

Starr and I had much to settle; we'd parted in anger and before I'd shared my true feelings, that I loved her and would stand by her no matter what.

One arm still in a sling, I raised the other to try to quiet them. "People, please!" I shouted over the din. "Listen to me!"

"Send the females back to Terra!" a man shouted.

"Nobody is going back to Terra!" I snapped. "How many of you have broken rules? Or failed to contribute to the storehouse? Or taken more than your share? Perhaps drunk too much ale and started a fight? Or attempted to woo another's mate?"

Several men shuffled their feet.

"Or caused dissension in the camp by inciting rivalries."

Gazes shifted to Icha, but then a man pushed his way through crowd. One of Icha's many lovers, Bork and I had butted heads over the running of the camp. "You cannot equate those wrongdoings with murder." He tore off his hood. A heavy forehead shadowed his eyes, but I could see his gaze flick to Icha before he turned to me. "Tell us, what crime *was* your mate convicted of?"

"She was falsely convicted. She is innocent of any and all crimes."

"Murder!" Icha shouted.

Bork bounded up onto the dais, overcrowding the platform. "The female must be banished!"

"Banish! Banish! Banish!" the crowd chanted.

Exile amounted to a death sentence. Starr couldn't survive the vast winter. She wouldn't be like Icha who'd been sheltered by the first tribe she approached. With the circumstance of Starr's arrival circulating at the camps, none of them would accept her. No one could survive for long in the frozen wilderness without a tribe.

"Expel the Terran! Expel the Terran!"

The animosity sparked a horrific thought: had one of my own tribe members set the traps at the meeting place? Had they tried to murder my mate?

"Stop!" I roared. "My mate's name is Starr!" They had talked with her, interacted with her around camp. And now they called her "the Terran?" Public sentiment shifted faster than the wind, and blew even colder.

The greatest shame was that I, too, for an instant, had felt the same way. Hadn't I condemned her at first?

I did not have time to convince my tribe with reason or merit. Anger intensified with every second. I could use the power of my position to control the outcome. Later, when emotions cooled, I could begin to win their hearts again. "I am tribal leader, and I will not banish Starrconner. If anyone disagrees with that, you are free to find yourself another tribe."

"You have banished others," Bork said.

"I exiled them knowing other tribes would shelter them."

"Then you must step down as leader."

"I won't do that, either. I have led this tribe nobly and capably." If I stepped down, the new chief would banish Starr. We would leave together, then, but I would not allow it to come to that.

"Then you leave us no choice." Bork squared his shoulders. "I challenge you to a *muta*!" He jabbed me twice in the upper chest—my bad shoulder. It wasn't a full-on punch, but he put more power into the ritualized gesture than required to signify a formal challenge of leadership. From the first chant, I'd expected a challenge, so I braced for it and took the blows without a wince, but it hurt.

"In accordance with our custom, the muta must occur before sundown," Bork said.

I peered at the midday sky. "I will rejoin you here in one hour." Better to face this head-on, get it over

251

with, and return to normal. But, first, I needed to see Starr to reassure myself she was all right.

Bork didn't fool me. He'd challenged me as much for the banishment of Icha as Starr's supposed crime. But I would win this. My injured shoulder wouldn't help, but it wouldn't hinder me, either. Stovak the healer would have to patch me up again afterward.

Darq shook his head and slipped away. I hoped he had the sense not to tell Starr about the muta. If she got an inkling I planned to strip to my leggings and knuckle it out in the freezing air, she'd have a fit. At least I hoped so. I wanted to believe she still cared about me, despite my poor behavior.

"We will fight," I told Bork, and then addressed the tribe. "When I win, you will accept the results."

Winning the challenge was only the first step. I would still need to earn back the support of my tribe and patch things up with Starr. Then I had to work with Enoki, Groman, and Loka to capture whoever had set those traps and prepare for the arrival of more females. Would more of them improve the situation or worsen it? Would the men still be as eager for mates? Would they hold it against the ones who were?

The crowd began to disperse. Bork shot a look of longing at Icha. *I'm doing this for you*, his glance seemed to say. How could someone as perfidious and fickle as she inspire such loyalty? The men longed for females; until Starr had come along, I'd been filled with as much yearning as any of them. They had to understand that Terra offered our civilization hope. I couldn't let someone like Icha destroy our chance.

I needed to prepare for the future. Starr and I would have a long talk. There could be no secrets between us. To ward off future confrontations like this one, I had to have all the information.

Chapter Nineteen

Starr

I was still seething when Darq reentered the cave.

"What's happening out there?" I asked. We'd heard rumbling and shouts, and, after securing my promise to stay put, Torg's brother had gone to investigate.

"He has been challenged to a muta," Darq replied.

"What's that?"

"A competition to determine who will lead the tribe."

"Are you saying he could lose the chiefdom?"

"If he loses the fight, he will no longer be leader."

"It's a fight? What kind of fight?"

"Two men strip down to their leggings and battle it out. The last one standing wins."

"That's how leadership is determined? That's crazy."

"Not so crazy. Simple. The challenge rarely occurs, but it is respected. The people will accept the result."

"When is the fight?"

"In an hour."

I shook my head. "Torg can't fight. He was shot with an arrow."

"I wondered why his arm was in a sling." Darq paced. "Bork is one of the brawlers in the camp. He is rash, and not very smart. Torg could beat him, but if he's injured...Bork would make a terrible leader."

"This Bork is the challenger?"

Darq twisted his mouth and nodded. "One of Icha's former paramours."

Her again. "What did I ever do to her? I didn't take her man; she already had one when I showed up!"

"Torg banished her because of you. It rankled that he didn't take her to warm his kel, but accepted you. Icha had objected to the exchange program. Without competition, she is the queen, and all the men are her subjects. She dislikes losing."

"Well, she might have a second chance. Torg doesn't want me anymore."

"He still wants you. That's why he's fighting for you."

"He's trying to keep his tribe," I muttered. Torg had made his feelings about me crystal clear.

"The people demanded he expel you. He refused. And because he refused, he was challenged."

He refused? Maybe we had a chance after all! "He can't fight with one arm. He could be injured." What if he hurt himself over me? His arm might never be the same, and he would lose control of his tribe. I wanted Torg to love me, believe me, but not at this cost. "I can't let him do that."

"Do what?" Torg stood there. He looked at me, his gaze searching, no longer angry.

"You can't fight Bork."

He glowered at Darq.

"You have one good arm—" I said.

He slipped off the sling and threw it. "Now I have two."

"Taking off the sling doesn't fix your arm," I snapped. Out of the corner of my eye, I saw Darq slipping away. Smart men and cowards knew when to vanish.

"There is nothing wrong with my arm." He flexed it, and I winced even though he didn't.

"Your shoulder, then." Spare me the male ego. "At least postpone the fight."

"I can't. When a chief is challenged, the muta must be settled before sundown."

"That's a stupid custom." Why couldn't he see reason?

"I didn't come to fight with you, Starconner. I came to apologize. I'm sorry for the way I reacted in the wood. You are not a murderess." He moved close to me, peered into my eyes, and stroked a gentle finger across my cheek. "Of that, I am certain. I was blindsided, and I acted badly. Can you forgive me?"

"Oh, Torg!" I flung my arms around him, avoiding his injured shoulder. Regardless of his insistence, he had been hurt. "Of course, I do." I sniffed tears. "I should have told you the truth at the start. All of this could have been prevented."

"Perhaps, perhaps not. We cannot undo the past; we can only move forward."

I hugged him, burying my face against his kel. Through the thick fur, I could hear his heart thump. He was such a good man. Forgiving. Kind. Brave. Strong.

And stubborn and injured. I lifted my head. "Are you sure the muta can't be postponed? Surely, being wounded is a mitigating factor."

He snorted. "The injury was a *decisive* factor. Bork believes he'll have an advantage."

"But—"

Someone cleared his throat. "Excuse me..." A tribe member of Loka's stood there. Seriously, Dakon needed some doors. Walking in unannounced had to stop.

Torg and I broke apart. "Did you find more traps?" he asked.

"No. We're certain we got them all. The meeting place is safe. I came with a message for Starr." He held out a piece of parchment.

I frowned. "A message? From who?"

"Groman's mate."

"Andrea?" I took the parchment and unrolled it.

Starr,

I'm at the meeting place. You got a reply from Maridelle. Come as soon as you can. Important!

-Andrea

"What does it say?" Torg asked.

"Andrea says I received a message from Maridelle, my attorney—my defender on Terra," I amended, unsure if he knew what a lawyer was. Dakonians settled disputes with fist fights and banishment, not legal wrangling. "She says I should go to the meeting place as soon as possible."

"If there's nothing else…" the messenger said.

"Tell Andrea I'll be there—"

"In the morning," Torg cut in. "I have to be here for the muta, otherwise I would take you now."

"I can go by myself. I can find the way."

"No. I'll take you." He motioned to the messenger. "Relay to Groman's mate that Starrconner will meet her in the morning." He dismissed the messenger.

The man left.

"Andrea said it was important!" I protested.

"Do you think it's so urgent it can't wait a little longer?" he asked.

I'd instructed Maridelle not to proceed with the appeal, but what if it had already been granted? Or been denied? The latter was more likely. Since I'd decided to stay, there was nothing I would do in the former case, and nothing I *could* do in the latter one. But still. If only Andrea had told me what Maridelle had said!

I sighed. "I guess it can wait—and now I can attend the muta."

"Absolutely not."

"Why?" This muta thing could change his life, our lives, and I couldn't be there?

"I want you to remain here."

"There aren't spectators?"

"There are, but having you watch would distract me. I need to focus on Bork."

I didn't like being banned, but I understood his

reasoning. He'd be fighting with a handicap and would need all his concentration. "All right. I'll stay here."

"Good. Thank you." Torg kissed me and then leaned his forehead against mine. "We will talk more, settle this unpleasantness, and then we will couple."

"That sounds like a good plan." I caressed one of his horns.

He growled and captured my hand. "You tease me."

"Only because I love you. You're my mate."

"You're *my* mate." His eyes darkened. "I love you, too.

* * * *

Torg left, and I paced the cave. He'd insisted he could handle Bork, but I worried. I should be at the muta, but I didn't want to do anything to cause him to lose the fight. He needed to keep his head in the game—or the muta, as it were. I didn't wish him to think I didn't have faith in him, but what if he lost the challenge and control of his tribe? He would be devastated. He derived pride and honor from his position, and he was a fair, progressive leader. The stupid tribe needed him!

Worse, what if Bork *physically* hurt him? It would take more than a few magic herbs to heal him. He was already injured and would be fighting with a handicap. The muta was the dumbest idea I'd heard of since the Terran-Dakon Exchange Program. Thanks to Andrea's foresight, Dakon would have a hospital, but it wouldn't come to fruition soon enough to help Torg. We needed medical equipment and supplies stat! Andrea and I would push development in the right direction, but it would take time to bring the planet up to the present day.

I hated this! Torg had banned me from the muta—and I couldn't go see Andrea.

I unrolled and reread her note. *Come as soon as you can. Important.* It had to refer to the appeal. What else could it be? Truth? I wanted to clear my name! What had happened to me wasn't fair. My government had asked for my help. I gave it, and when I ran into trouble, they deserted me. Torg wouldn't surrender the tribe to a disgruntled member, and I didn't like giving up, either. I resented how my government had blackened my reputation—even if no one had known my name before the unfortunate judicial encounter.

I swung my arms as I stalked back and forth in the cave. In reality, a retrial wasn't an option I could pursue. The judicial process could take months—in addition to the time required to get to Earth. I would hate to be separated from Torg that long, and he couldn't accompany me. If he left, somebody would stage a coup, and he'd lose his tribe.

A retrial offered only a second chance, not a guarantee of acquittal. If the conviction was upheld, I could end up in prison again. I couldn't count on the government sending me back. So I had to stay put.

Unless...the retrial could be conducted via vid-con with me in absentia? Hmm...Dakon had the link up. Trials were mostly electronic anyway. Only the defense and prosecution were required to appear in person; the judge and jury were beamed in holographically. They could beam me in, couldn't they? I'd agree to a vid trial—it was a no-lose scenario. If I won, my name got cleared; if I lost, I'd be safe on Dakon. All things being equal, I'd prefer to not have my name footnoted in the annals of history with the tag "murderer."

What if Maridelle needed a quick response from me to make that happen? Maybe she had a limited window of opportunity to set the process in motion.

If Andrea recommended I contact Maridelle ASAP, I should. She was as sharp as a laser pistol. Perceptive. I trusted her and Tessa. We three had bonded, and they'd become like sisters to me.

I shouldn't have acquiesced to Torg's request. I

nibbled a fingernail. I could find my way to the meeting place. There was plenty of time to hike there and back by dark. Torg would be furious, and I should avoid upsetting him so soon after our first argument and the muta, but I had to go with my gut, and my gut said go.

Torg was being overprotective by insisting on escorting me. The meeting place was free of booby traps. Andrea and Groman would be there, and probably Tessa and Loka, too, so I wouldn't be alone.

But I couldn't just disappear. Torg would worry.

"Do you need anything before I go?" Darq halted in the main room and pulled on his kel. He got to watch the muta! Well, I had other things to do, like clear my name. I'd been wronged, terribly wronged, and now I could make it right.

A solution to my problem took shape. "Um, yeah, you could do me a favor. Hang on a sec."

I grabbed Torg's pack and pulled out three sheets of parchment. "Torg was going to teach me your language. Would you write a few phrases for me so I can practice while everyone is gone?"

"Sure. What do you want me to write?"

"Let me think...um...okay, how about how about 'I need to tan some kel hide.'"

264

Darq scrawled some incomprehensible symbols on the paper and handed it to me. I set it aside and handed him a fresh sheet. I soothed my guilt over wasting such a precious commodity with the rationalization Andrea and I could add paper to the shipment. I'd have her do that right after I found out what Maridelle wanted. Earth people rarely used paper, but Andrea would be able to scare up some. "Write, 'it's very cold outside,'" I directed Darq.

He scratched the quill across the sheet. The sentence didn't look any different from the other one. When I tried to learn the language for real, it would be a challenge. I placed the weather report with the other sheet.

"Last one. 'I went to the meeting place.'" Would Darq catch on? My heart thumped. If he got an inkling of what I was up to, he'd rat me out in an instant.

He dipped the quill into the ink.

I released my breath silently.

"Thank you." I set the sheet separate from the others so I wouldn't get them mixed up.

"You're welcome. If that's all, I'll be off. The muta will start soon." He headed toward the exit.

"Darq?"

He looked at me.

"Torg will be okay, won't he? I couldn't stand it if something happened to him." Doubts about the wisdom of sneaking away assailed me. Torg, the stubborn man, needed me. He might think he was invincible, but he wasn't.

Darq smiled. "Don't worry. Torg will come home with a few bruises, but he'll be fine. It will be over soon." He waved and left.

I waited for his footsteps to recede. As I turned from the table, I caught the leg, and it teetered. Ink pot, quill, and parchment started to slide. I grabbed for the notes Darq had written, but they, along with everything else, landed on the floor. Ink spilled into the dirt.

No, no, no. I snatched up the dirtied, smudged parchments. Which sheet was the right one?

Did the ink look a little fresher on this one? That had to be it, and if it wasn't, there was nothing I could do about it.

I sprinted to our private chamber, placed the note on our bed, and shoved the other two parchment sheets underneath the hides. I would practice writing those sentences—at a later date.

I needed to hurry. The sooner I got there, the sooner I could get back to Torg. If I went now, he wouldn't have to go in the morning—and I had a strong feeling he wouldn't be up to it. How much could a man take?

I pulled on my kel and crept out the back way so Torg and Darq wouldn't see me.

* * * *

Please still be here. Please still be here. I hop-ran across the snow to the lodge and charged inside. "I'm here!"

Andrea, seated in front of the computer, spun around. Grim anxiety furrowed her brow. "Thank goodness. The messenger said you weren't coming until tomorrow. Where's Torg?"

"At camp. It's a long story. I'll tell you later. What did Maridelle say? Is it about the appeal?"

Her eyes bugged out a little. "You came alone?"

"I know the way."

She pressed a hand to her throat. "You need to read Maridelle's message." Her fingers flew over the screen. "Here."

I peered over her shoulder.

Dear Starr,

Thank the gods, I heard from you. The SS Australia is returning to Dakon to pick you up. You are in grave danger. The Carmichaels ordered a hit.

267

Alien Mate

The Terran Organized Crime Unit believes they placed an assassin aboard the ship.

An assassin? On the ship? There was a hit on me? My knees buckled. I could almost feel the red eye of the laser rifle beading on my skull. There was more to Maridelle's message, but two words overshadowed the rest. *Hit. Assassin.*

A lot has happened since you left. With the information you provided to the TOCU, they arrested the underbosses and Jaxon's brother, Rogerio. He also was indicted for Jaxon's murder. Forensics restored deleted vid footage from Jaxon's office. The vid showed Rogerio entering the office after you and killing Jaxon. They were fighting over control of the organization. Your conviction has been set aside, and your name has been cleared.

There was a hit on me?

As I said, the ship has been ordered back to Dakon. The TOCU will take you into protective custody. I'm so sorry. Try to stay safe until it arrives. Please check in often to let me know you're okay.

Maridelle.

I blinked at the screen, reread the message, and read it again. A hit. Assassin aboard. My name had been cleared. How little that mattered in light of my imminent death.

If sending me billions of miles away to an alien planet couldn't save me, what the hell could protective custody do? What a joke. The Carmichaels intended to kill me.

"Starr, are you okay? Starr?" Andrea's voice drifted in from a long way off.

My joints and limbs seemed to be connected by loose rubber bands. It was amazing I could manage to stand upright. Even more astounding, I was still alive. Why hadn't they killed me yet? What were they waiting for?

"Why didn't you tell me what was in her message?" I croaked.

"I should have. I realized that as soon as the messenger left. But I panicked. I didn't know how to tell you! How could I write that in a note? It never occurred to me you would come alone. I thought for sure Torg would accompany you. I really screwed up. I'm sorry."

"It's not your fault." Nothing Andrea or anybody did could make a difference now. I would hit the snow deader than dead before Torg could grab a bow. I was a walking target. The Carmichael hit men were sharpshooters with the most advanced weapons available.

Andrea touched my elbow. "Are you all right?"

My mouth and head fuzzed. "Y-yeah." No. Of course, I wasn't all right! *Focus, Starr, focus. Focus and you might get to live another nanosecond.*

"I'm as stunned as you are." Doubtful. Her concern was genuine, but *her* life wasn't threatened—not unless she stood too close to me, and not even then, because Carmichael hit men never missed a shot. Why wasn't I dead yet?

"After I saw the message, while I waited for you to arrive," Andrea continued, "I kept hammering at my brain, trying to come up with a suspect. I reviewed the ship manifests and logs. The passenger manifest listed fifty women and ten crew members for a total of sixty persons. However, the ship's housekeeping robo maintained sixty-one cabins."

"An extra person? The assassin?"

She nodded. "I think so."

"Why didn't he kill me on board? Not that I'm complaining, you understand."

"No getaway. He had nowhere to escape to as long as we were on the ship. He would have to eliminate all the witnesses and that meant the crew, too—and then how would he get back?"

"So he got off the ship with us and has been lying in wait for the right moment."

Andrea looked solemn. "That would be my guess."

"But where would he have gone? He couldn't pass himself off as a female. Not for long, anyway." I flung out an arm. "How could he survive the cold? What would he do for food? How would he get home?"

"Starr...he has everything he needs right here. The emergency huts. The larder. He's probably been holed up here the entire time. My guess is he plans to hitch a ride home on the next ship."

"And you let me come here?" I squeaked.

"I didn't think about that until after I'd sent the messenger. But, I think it's safe now. When Loka's men swept the compound for traps, they checked all the buildings. They probably scared off the assassin."

Two simultaneous thoughts invaded my brain: Carmichael hit men didn't scare off, and now we had two assassins running around. One born and raised on Dakon and one imported. Of the two, I feared the latter the most. I'd rushed over here, practically delivered myself right into the assassin's hands. Between my shoulder blades, my skin crawled as if a red laser eye drilled into my back right now. Slowly, I pivoted to peer behind me. Nobody. The flap over the door swayed from the swirling wind. I should be barricaded in a fortress in which only I knew the entry pass codes, and instead, I was on a planet that didn't have *doors* on its huts.

"I'm so sorry," Andrea said. "I saw Maridelle's message and sent Loka's guy after you. Then I dug into the ship's records."

"How am I going to get to camp?" I whispered, wishing I was in the cave, buried under a pile of kel hides where the bogeyman couldn't see me. Rational thought wasn't my strong suit right now. Torg could place guards outside the cave, but the hit man would pick them off and march right in like everyone else did.

What the hell was I going to do?

"Groman and Loka are here; they'll take you to Torg."

Their presence wouldn't prevent the assassin from taking me out. I flexed my shoulders to shake off the creepy-crawly sensation.

If I returned to camp, I'd be endangering Torg's life, Darq's, and everyone else's. "I need to think. To come up with a plan."

Andrea rubbed her neck. "I wonder why they didn't kill you back on Terra?"

"Because they kept me in isolation, away from the

other inmates, and the guards dogged me every second of the day. They never took their eyes off me," I recalled. At the time, I'd assumed they'd been there to intimidate me. Had they been charged with protecting me?

"That's what we need to do, then. Keep you guarded until the ship gets here." She powered down the system. It blinked and went dark. A metaphor for my near future.

The assassin wouldn't let me board the vessel and fly away. Crew members had no bodyguard training. They were stewards, coordinators, navigators. If by some fluke I arrived on Terra, well, hello, there'd be more hit men lined up waiting for me.

At least here, there was only the one.

Outside this lodge, he waited for me. Stalked me. I could feel it. Every step, every move might be my last; my very existence was booby trapped like the town had been.

Booby trapped.

What if... "Andrea...maybe the hit man set those booby traps for me?"

"Why would a professional hit man bother with bows and arrows? Why not shoot you with a laser pistol?"

"Because the energy cartridges went dead from the cold," said a familiar voice.

Tessa stood there holding an LP. "But have no worry." She waved the laser pistol at the computer. "After Andrea got the system up, I was able to recharge them."

"Tessa? What are you doing?" Dumb question, but my mind could not comprehend the images my eyes were seeing. Not Tessa. She was one of *us*. We were friends. She and Andrea were like family. Tessa? Giggly, slightly loopy, bubbly Tessa?

Pop went the bubbles. Standing before me gripping a weapon was a cold-eyed, emotionless killer.

"Why would you do this?" Andrea asked.

"Nothing personal, ladies. It's just a job."

Tessa would kill us both. She had to. She couldn't off me and leave an eyewitness.

Little clues fell into place. She'd led the little tour of the town, nudging us toward the booby-trapped huts. At the apothecary, at the last minute she'd fallen back, supposedly to talk to Loka, allowing me to move forward and trigger the trip wire. She'd insisted on accompanying him when he'd gone to check the meeting place for more traps. Circumstantial evidence, but it all made sense now.

"Was anything real?" I asked. She'd seemed taken with Loka. She'd bounced with excitement when they'd left the lodge after he'd chosen her. She'd acted so happy. They often hugged. She'd comforted me after Torg had been shot—by the traps she'd set. Her emotions had been as fraudulent as her manufactured past.

The assassin smirked. "There was a Tessa Chartreuse who laundered money through her escort service, but she had a little accident en route to the *SS Australia.*"

"You killed her?" I mourned the Tessa I never met, a woman whose life had been snuffed out because of me.

The assassin aimed the LP at my forehead.

My bladder released. If I hadn't stopped in the woods, I would have peed myself. Begging was humiliating enough. "Don't, please..."

I'd never see Torg again. My sexy, strong alien mate. Who was at this moment fighting to keep me in camp. Oh why hadn't I waited until morning like he asked? Maybe Tessa-not-Tessa wouldn't have revealed herself if Torg had been with me. *Oh, Torg, I'm so sorry.* We'd never get to make little Terran-Dakonian babies.

275

Neither would Andrea. After the assassin eliminated me, she'd kill her. "I'm sorry, Andrea."

Oomph!

Andrea's foot connected with the pistol, and it arced through the air. The assassin bared her teeth and struck at Andrea's throat. She deflected the blow with her forearm and delivered an undercut to the assailant's jaw, snapping her head.

The assassin stumbled but recovered her footing, and lunged. Trading kicks and blows, they flew at each other. Where had Andrea learned to fight like that? She was *lethal*.

I had to do something! I had to help! But I was no fighter. One hit or kick would put me down for the count. The weapon! I swept my gaze over the lodge. In the corner!

The LP felt solid, heavy, and awkward in my hand, and I feared I'd discharge it just by holding it. Andrea could do everything, but I couldn't tell which end of the laser weapon was up. Well, I did know that, but it was all I could figure out.

Andrea hooked her arm around the hit woman's neck and squeezed. Tessa turned red and tried to dislodge Andrea's arm, but, in seconds, she passed out. Andrea dropped the limp body and flexed her skinned, bruised knuckles. I gaped, still in shock at the way she had defended herself—still stunned that Tessa was a Carmichael hit woman.

"Good gods," I choked out. "You saved my life. Our lives. Where did you learn to fight like that?"

"In the military. Special Forces. The hacking came later." She eyed the weapon in my hand. "You're holding that all wrong. Do you mind if I take it?" She jutted her jaw at the body. "She'll come to in few minutes, and I'd rather not fight her again." Andrea shook her bruised hand.

Quickly, I passed her the laser pistol. Gripping it like a pro, Andrea leveled a gaze on me. "I took a risk when I kicked the LP. It could have discharged and killed you. But she intended to kill us both, anyway, so I figured we had nothing to lose."

"Hey, I'm good with it," I said.

The assassin gave a little moan.

"I'll get something to tie her up," I offered.

"Good idea. Try the trading post. Get Groman, too. It won't hurt to have a little extra muscle. He should be in the apothecary, refilling supplies he used on Torg. What are we going to tell Loka?"

"He'll be devastated." Like Torg and Groman would have been if the Tessa imposter had succeeded in murdering me and Andrea. I wished Torg were here. I needed him. I eyed the hit woman. "What are we going to do with her?"

Andrea lifted a shoulder. "We'll have to keep her locked up somehow until the ship arrives. After you bring some restraints, I'll notify your Maridelle we have the hit woman in custody." She raised the gun at little. "At least we have a weapon."

"She probably has a stash."

"You're right. We'll have them search her camp."

"Let me get the ties and Groman. You've got it under control here." My legs still felt rubbery, but I hurried from the lodge.

The air was frigid as always, but hyped up on adrenalin, I hardly noticed as I ran for the apothecary. Better to get Groman first. Although Andrea was armed and capable, I didn't like leaving her alone with a professional assassin.

I burst into the apothecary. "Groman!" Not there. No telling where he would have gone next. The trading post? I needed to go there anyway.

I raced along the line of huts. All the traps had been found, but the fluffy ground cover made me nervous. Who knew what was hidden under all the snow? What if Loka and his tribe mates had missed a

278

trap? *They found them all. Andrea has Tessa. You're being paranoid.* However, considering what I'd been through, I had a right to be.

Outside the trading post, I stomped the snow off my boots. Head down, I noticed the man from the corner of my eye.

He emerged from around the side of the hut.

I looked up.

First to register: his synthetic mottled white-off-white subzero bodysuit, perfect camouflage in the snow. Second: his Terran features. Third, his laser pistol.

Fourth: what Andrea had mentioned, and we'd both forgotten in the scuffle with the fake Tessa: "The passenger manifest listed fifty women and ten crewmembers for a total of sixty persons. However, the ship's housekeeping robo maintained sixty-one cabins."

The crew had been accounted for, and Tessa had been one of the fifty women, so that left one extra cabin for one extra passenger.

Tessa had a partner. How flattering the Carmichaels considered me significant enough to double-team me. Of course, the line between flattery and terror was thin. Very thin.

The assassin's red nose ran from the cold, and his lips were chapped, but his eyes were deadly.

Andrea had saved my ass the last time; this time, I was a goner.

I inched backward as if I could sneak some distance between us and then make a run for it. Where the hell was Groman? The messenger who'd come to camp? Loka? He'd accompanied the fake Tessa, hadn't he? I didn't dare take my eyes off the hit man and his weapon to check.

A predator toying with his prey, he let me creep several steps before closing the distance. For the second time that day, my bladder released involuntarily, and this time urine did trickle out. Backing up some more, I tripped over something half buried in the snow.

Loka's body. Blood seeped from a hole between his eyes, open to the sky.

I screamed.

The assassin aimed at my head.

Whoosh!

The LP discharged into the ground as an arrow pierced his throat.

Chapter Twenty

Torg

My mate screamed. As the man fell, his weapon emitted a noise and a flash of light. I raced to Starr who lay next to Loka's body. Had she been injured? I'd waited for the best opening, but when the man raised his weapon, it was then or never. I'd released the arrow and severed his windpipe.

I pulled Starr into my arms and ran my hands inside her kel, over her body. No injuries. My hands shook with relief.

Gurgles erupted from the dying man's throat. His blood darkened the snow.

"Oh gods, Torg," she sobbed. "I c-c-an't believe you're here."

"Of course, I'm here. I came for you. It's okay. You're safe." I stroked her soft yellow hair, surveyed Loka's body and the Terran. Who was he?

I'd found the note after the muta. I couldn't believe she'd left camp after promising not to, after the meeting place had been rigged. Anger at her impetuousness evaporated the instant I'd emerged from the trees to see the man in strange clothes threatening her. I didn't recognize his weapon, but knew it was one, and he intended harm. My shoulder had taken quite a beating in the muta, but pain ceased to matter as I loaded an arrow into a bow.

Starr pushed at my chest and scrubbed her face with her tiny hands. "We have to help Andrea. She's in the meeting place with Tes—the other assassin."

Another assassin? I leaped to my feet. "You stay here—"

The gurgles had ceased, and the man's sightless eyes stared at the gray sky. He had lived for only a couple of minutes after I shot him, but I took comfort that he had suffered and known he was going to die. Nobody threatened my mate.

Starr grabbed my sleeve. "Andrea's okay. She's in control; she's guarding Tessa. She needs restraints."

"Wait a minute—Loka's mate? I don't understand."

"Tessa didn't come to be his mate. Not for real. She and that man"—she pointed to the dead Terran—"were sent by the Carmichaels to kill me. They set the traps for me." She choked a little. "One of them killed Loka."

282

"He was a good man." His assistance last night when I'd been shot had saved lives. He'd found the other traps before we'd walked into them. Many would mourn him, myself included.

Starr retrieved the weapon from the snow.

It was like nothing I'd ever seen, neither wood nor stone, but a dull-gray material with buttons on the sides and a grip that fit in one's palm attached to a slender barrel. "What is that?"

"It's called a laser pistol. It shoots a concentrated beam of light."

"And that's dangerous?" How could light be harmful?

"Lethal." Grimacing, she patted the man's sides and pulled out some small gray rectangles from his pockets.

"What are those?"

"Energy cartridges for the weapon." She stood and jutted her chin at the trading post. "Let's go inside."

In the trading post, we cut strips from a kel hide. As we left the hut, Groman emerged from the trees, and I waved him over. "Come with us," I called.

He spotted the bodies and swore. "Is that Loka? And a Terran?" He knelt in the snow beside the bodies.

"They're dead," I said.

But he checked anyway. "They are. What happened?"

"We'll explain on the way to the lodge. Come, your mate is waiting."

In a few short sentences, Starr filled him in. "Andrea told me you'd be in the apothecary. I went to look for you there."

"I wanted to check the area among the trees. Look for more clues. But the snow covered everything."

Tessa sat on the lodge floor, guarded by Andrea who aimed a weapon like the one Starr had confiscated from the dead Terran. If I hadn't met Loka's mate before, I wouldn't have recognized her. Her countenance had become hard and cold. If her gaze had been a weapon, we would all be dead.

Andrea glanced at Starr. "What took you so long?"

Starr gestured with her weapon. "Tessa had a friend. Remember that extra cabin? I ran into the stowaway outside."

Andrea's jaw dropped. "What happened?"

"Torg killed him."

Tessa remained silent.

"Either he or she"—Starr pointed at Tessa—"killed Loka. I tripped over his body."

Andrea raked a hard gaze over her captive. "Did

284

you kill him?"

She took so long to answer, for a moment, I didn't think she was going to reply. "No," she said finally. "Dimitri must have caught him coming out of one of the huts."

Andrea pointed the strange weapon at Tessa. A bead of red light appeared between her eyebrows. "These men are going to tie you up. If I see so much as a muscle twitch, I'll shoot."

Groman and I secured her wrists and ankles with the kel strips.

"Tying her is a short-term solution," Starr said. "It will take a couple of weeks for the ship to get here." She planted her hands on her hips. "I don't suppose Dakon has a jail?"

"Not one she can't walk out of. But we'll devise something. We need to inform Enoki."

I remained with the females while Groman went to get the council chief. Andrea and Starr got on the computer and sent a message to her defender on Terra.

Enoki arrived with three men. The council chief looked as grim as I'd ever seen him. "I will make sure she does not escape," he vowed.

"You should have a good weapon." Andrea showed

him how to operate the *laser pistol*. Simple, really. I insisted on keeping the other one. My mate had been the one targeted, and the superiority of the laser pistol over the bow and arrow was clear—although the latter had felled the assassin.

Starr twisted her hands. "I feel responsible for Loka's death. If I hadn't been here, Tessa and Dimitri wouldn't have come, and he would still be alive."

"You didn't kill Loka. Dimitri did," Andrea said.

"That's true," I agreed. "If the tribe dares to say one word against you, they'll deal with me." I'd fight as many battles or mutas as I had to.

"You are still chief, then?"

"Yes. Our camp healer is busy tending to my challenger's injuries." I omitted the healer had wanted to tend to me, too, but I'd hurried after my wayward mate. Thank the fates, I had. And now, with Bork in his place, others might be discouraged from challenging my leadership—today, anyway.

"At least I don't have that on my conscience." Starr touched a bruise on my cheek. Bork had gotten in a couple of good punches, but I'd defeated him. "You had to fight because of me."

"I protect my mate. It is nothing any other man wouldn't have done."

Groman and Enoki nodded.

"He speaks the truth," Enoki said. "Under the circumstances, though, we will need to reevaluate the exchange program."

"About that." Andrea planted her hands on her hips. "Starr and I have a plan. Dakon could benefit a whole lot more from the arrangement than it is right now."

"Earth women would love Dakonian men, but Terra One World is coercing the ones who have little choice," Starr said. "The Earth government might seek to get rid of more people like Tessa."

"Starr and I would like to renegotiate the treaty. We can get you supplies, equipment, *and* mates."

"We will talk later." Enoki nodded. "For now, I must ward this Terran female and notify Loka's tribe of his death."

After they left, Starr hugged me, slipping her hands inside my kel to squeeze my waist. I winced as a sharp pain shot through me. She withdrew. "What's wrong?"

"Nothing."

"It's not nothing. Let me see."

"No, it's all right."

But she grabbed the front of my kel and undid the

toggles. "You're bleeding again!"

I suspected I had a broken rib, too, but I wasn't about to tell her.

To my humiliation, she insisted Groman patch me up again. "This is getting to be a habit," he said.

"Not one I like," I muttered.

* * * *

"Now, let us talk," I said when we'd arrived at the cave and removed our kels.

To my mate's credit, she didn't pretend to misunderstand. "I'm sorry." She hung her head. "I shouldn't have run off like that."

"No. You tricked Darq into helping you." Fortunately, she hadn't been very good at it. Upon returning from the muta, I found the message in Darq's hand on my bed of kels: *it's very cold outside.* An odd note for him to write since everyone already knew that, and I'd passed him in the main chamber and he'd made no mention of it then. I showed him the note, and he'd told me of Starr's request.

My mate hung her head. "That was wrong of me, too."

"I couldn't stand it if anything happened to you, Starrconner. I saw that man holding the weapon, and I about died. If I'd arrived at the meeting place a minute later..."

On my way out of the cave to retrieve my wayward mate, I'd grabbed an artillery set to fulfill my promise to Loka. If I hadn't thought to grab it...

"I won't do it again. But I had such a strong feeling I had to see Andrea right away."

I stalked toward her and cupped her face. "If you have strong feelings, you need to tell me."

"I love you. That's my strong feeling."

Warmth suffused my chest and lower. "I love you, too." I enfolded her in my arms and kissed her eyelids, her nose, her cheeks, and finally, her mouth. Her lips parted, and I drank in her sweetness, savoring her exotic taste. Our bond could never be broken. I felt her in every cell of my being: my head, my heart, my groin. My cock thickened.

Seeing her alive wasn't enough. I needed tactile reassurance.

I severed contact long enough to strip out of my clothes.

"What are you doing?" she asked.

"I am disrobing." I flashed her my most innocent smile before I hugged her tight. I cupped her rounded buttocks and pulled her against my rising need.

Her breath caught in her throat, but she did not

react as I'd hoped. She resisted with a frown. "This isn't a good idea."

"Why not?" I bent my head to nibble the slope of her neck. She shivered. Victory.

"You're injured."

I sucked on her earlobe. "It's just a scratch."

"Torg, please," she protested, but arched her neck.

"Please, more? Okay." I kissed a slow trail to the other side and cupped her breasts, strumming her hardening nipples with my thumbs.

She lifted her shoulder, twisting away from my mouth. "I'm serious. I saw your wound when Groman patched you up again. The bruises to your ribs. Now, be good."

Her concern for my welfare spread warmth through my chest. Her heart was in the right place, even if her hands were nowhere close to where I wanted them. I whispered in her ear, "I promise, I'll be very good." I walked her backward to a table. Before she could utter a word, I grabbed her tunic and stripped it off her then tugged on her leggings.

She locked her knees to keep me from pulling them all the way off. I dropped to my knees to kiss her mons, her soft, rounded tummy. "You're impossible!" Her eyes sparked with mock anger, and desire. "If you hurt yourself, it will be all on you," she huffed.

If I hurt myself, it would be worth it. "I'll take full responsibility." I tugged her leggings to her ankles, and she kicked them aside. I hid a smile of triumph by teasing her pleasure nub with the curled tip of my tongue. She stumbled and clutched at my shoulders, an opportunity I pressed to full advantage by licking her sex more avidly.

Her knees buckled with the first orgasm, but I held her up and continued enjoying my mate. As she neared the crest of the next peak, I bent her over the table and slid into her. Her channel was pure bliss around my cock. So slick. So warm. So tight.

Starr mewled, and I cupped her mons with one hand and stroked her pearl as I pumped inside her. Her womanhood quivered around my cock and then convulsed as rapture claimed her for a second time. It nearly undid me, but I held off until the tremors subsided, and then I grabbed her hips and took my pleasure with strong, powerful strokes. Lights exploded in my eyes when I climaxed, every nerve firing at once. I bellowed, crying out her name, my Starr, my only, my forever.

We stumbled to the bed where I pulled Starr into the crook of my body. Our spent passion scented the air. I covered her breast with my hand and nuzzled her neck.

Starr exhaled a contented sigh. "I give in to you too easily and too fast."

"I don't think that's possible," I replied.

She giggled. "I'm sure you don't." Then her mood sobered. She twisted in my arms and stroked my horns, sending a heated sensation clear down to my toes. The love in her soft blue eyes made my throat catch. "I would give you everything I have. You're my mate."

I remembered my anticipation the day she arrived. Though she hadn't been what I'd expected, we'd been meant for each other. Despite our rocky meeting, we'd bonded at the start. I could not imagine mating with anyone but Starr. "And you're mine. Forever and always."

Epilogue

Starr

Two solar rotations later

"How do I look?" Darq adjusted his kel for the third time.

Torg shrugged. "The same as always."

I shot him a censuring look and reassured Darq. "Very handsome." Seated on a high-backed divan, I shifted position and stretched out my legs. Getting comfortable was hard these days, but the baby would be born soon.

"You don't think I should wear Terran garments?" he asked.

I shook my head. "No. The women are coming to meet an alien man. They'll expect you to look as Dakonian as possible. Brush your hair back. Show off your horns. They'll love that."

Darq peered into the mirror I'd received in the last shipment of supplies and finger-combed his hair.

"Perfect." I flashed a thumbs-up.

"I shouldn't take the snow skimmer, then."

Alien Mate

Dakonians no longer had to trek on foot—not since Andrea and I had renegotiated the exchange program. We had Enoki inform Earth that since they'd seen fit to allow a dangerous criminal to be sent to Dakon, the shipment of illuvian ore would halt unless certain conditions were met. First, they had to stop sending convicts and open the program to all women. Second. A little reconstruction was in order. They had to bring the planet up to the present age. In the past year, fleets of ships had delivered supplies. But no women until today. It had taken time to retool the recruitment procedure.

This new group of women would arrive on a much different Dakon than the one Andrea, Tessa, and I had landed on. I still missed the woman I'd thought Tessa was. In the lodge when we'd announced Loka had been killed, for the briefest second, I imagined I'd seen a glint of regret in her eyes, but I knew better. There was only cold and darkness. You couldn't assassinate as many people as she had and retain your humanity. Murder killed both victim and perpetrator. The former lost his life, the latter his soul. Two years had passed since our arrival, and I'd taken to thinking of Tessa as two people because it was easier that way. There'd been our bubbly, cheerful shipmate, and there'd been the cold-eyed killer—who'd gone back to Terra to be convicted of first-degree murder and sentenced to life in prison without the possibility of parole.

I'd learned from Maridelle, with whom I had frequent vid contact, that in its own inept way, my former government had attempted to protect me. The hit had been ordered long before I left Terra. The murder charges and subsequent trial had been a farce, concocted by my government so they could send me out of reach of the Carmichaels.

We all knew how that had worked out.

The one hundred women soon to arrive had been vetted stringently. I'd written the screening procedures myself, and Andrea had hacked into the exchange program's recruitment protocols and planted them. One of the new arrivals would be Darq's mate. He'd drawn a chit.

"She'll prefer to ride by skimmer," I advised him. "Your female is coming for a Dakonian man, not a two tripta hike in the snow."

"Oh."

"Everything will be fine. You'll do great."

"Go already!" Torg yelled.

"Torg!"

"No, he's right." Darq straightened. "I will see you

295

later. When I return, it will be with my mate." He hurried from the cave.

"You were rather rude," I chided Torg. "He's nervous about the meeting—as I'm sure you were."

"Maybe a little," he admitted. "But I wanted to be alone with you and Starlet." He rubbed my swollen belly.

I, and many of the first arrivals—including Andrea—had proven definitively that Dakonians and Terrans were compatible and could reproduce. Andrea's baby would be born a month after ours. With as often as Torg and I had sex, I would have been pregnant a lot sooner, except for the contraceptive implant. Something else my former government had failed to plan for. More than three-quarters of the first arrivals were on birth control. After promising compatible, fertile mates, Earth had sent a group of women who *couldn't* bear children—at least not for a while. Without the tool to remove the implant, we had to wait for its efficacy to wear off. Andrea and I leveraged that little oversight in our negotiations, too.

"We can't call our daughter Starlet." We'd had many discussions but had not yet arrived at an agreement.

"Why not? Your name is Starr; she'll be our little

star."

"No." I shook my head.

"We could call her Icha, then," he said with a straight face.

I punched his arm lightly. "Don't you even—"

He laughed, and I did, too. My nemesis no longer represented a threat to me or anyone else. I learned that Tessa had told Icha of my conviction so word would spread, Torg's tribe would expel me, and I'd be forced out into the open. Time had taken care of Icha. She'd lost power as more and more couples gave birth to babies and program opponents decided they preferred a full-time Terran female over a once-in-a-while kel-warmer troublemaker.

I teased Torg, but he would get his way. The name Starlet had grown on me, and anything that made my mate happy, made me happy. I was pleased to have a healthy baby—and a real medical center nearby for the birth of my first child.

One whole shipment of insulated pre-fab housing panels had been used to construct a medical center. Another shipment had provided bio scanners, robo operators, osteoknitters, and other medical devices. Earth physicians and medical technicians provided consultation and training for the Dakonian healers.

I intended to have a home cave birth with Stovak attending, but having the medical center on standby and the skimmer to get there reassured me. It was at the med facility we'd learned the sex of our child. We'd considered waiting to find out in the time-honored manner, but since females were so important to the future, we decided we wanted to know.

Torg's expression turned serious. "Do you mind still living in the cave?"

Many Dakonians had moved into the pre-fab housing units. They were well insulated against draft and dampness and came with all the conveniences and comforts.

"No, it's your home. Our home," I amended. And it had been modified quite a bit. A composite material had been laid over the dirt floor. Space heaters fueled by energy packs warmed the chambers, although we supplemented with wood for atmosphere. I'd gotten used to having a roaring fire. Somewhere on Terra— maybe an antique shop—several woodstoves had been located and shipped to us. We built our fires in those, eliminating the smoke and soot. I owed Andrea for that one. She could find anything. She could locate a single tick in a herd of kel. If kel got ticks; I suspected it was too cold. One day, the Terrans would wake up to discover that half of everything they owned had been mysteriously transported to Dakon.

"Do you mind the way the cave has changed?" I asked him. It didn't look Dakonian anymore.

I'd furnished it as a Terran home with sofas, a huge massaging hover bed, lamps, artwork, and a full kitchen complete with a flash cooker, although I did none of the cooking. Torg and Darq took care of that. But hey, I wanted to make their lives easier.

"No." He squeezed my hand. "I'm humbled by what you've done for us. I did not think I would see this kind of progress in my lifetime. Before you came, we faced extinction. You, Andrea, and the other females gave us more than we could have dreamed of."

He took a deep breath and let it out. "Enoki has decided we should search for others, to see if descendants of asteroid survivors live on the other side of Dakon. Before, the warm season didn't last long enough for us to go on foot, but now we can travel in the vehicles. A team has volunteered to go."

"That's great news." I knew Torg and his brethren longed to reunite all their people.

He hugged me close to his warm body and rubbed my tummy. "We're going to call our daughter Starlet, right?"

"We'll see." I settled my head on his shoulder, reached up, and caressed his horns. He growled, and I giggled.

Starlet, I can't wait for you to meet your Daddy. I cuddled next to my alien mate and sighed with contentment.

* * *

Thank you for reading *Alien Mate (Alien Mate 1)*. Darq, Torg's brother, meets his mate, Sunny, in ***Alien Attraction*** (Alien Mate 2). Turn the page for an excerpt from their sizzling romance. FYI, besides the four books in the Alien Mate series, there is a spinoff series, Dakonian Alien Mail Order Brides. In that series, the Dakonian men join the Intergalactic Dating Agency and come to find their Fated Mates. You can find all those books listed at the end of this book. Finally, get your copy of a FREE Dakonian romance when you subscribe to my newsletter: https://carabristol.com/newsletter/.

Alien Attraction (Alien Mate 2)

Chapter One

Sunny

"Absolutely not! Have you lost your mind?" I glared across the desk, incredulous at what had popped out of my agent's mouth. The woman couldn't be serious. I'd been forced to perform some crazy stunts in my reality-show career, but this would take the cake.

"The ratings will go supernova," Chantelle Aubergine said with a straight face.

"I don't care about the ratings! This is my life we're talking about."

"You should care about the ratings—they keep you employed. Without good ratings, there would be no *Sunny Weathers' Excellent Adventures*."

Excellent adventures? What a crock. The reality show should be called *Stick It to Sunny* or *Test How Much We Can Throw at Sunny Before She Loses It*. The venture had started out as campy fun, but the stunts and segments had grown wilder and crazier. Now, I dreaded each new season.

"Sky diving, military boot camp, living in the jungle during monsoon season, working on a fishing boat, spending a month in the desert with the scorpions and snakes, I did it."

Chantelle chuckled. "Military boot camp. Hilarious! You and Stormy were great."

In the early years, my sister and I had teamed up to do the show, which had been called *Sunny and Stormy's Excellent Adventures*. Then Devon had come along and put a halt to her career. To keep viewers engaged, Apogee Productions had upped the ante, demanding longer, weirder *adventures*.

"I draw the line at marrying a purple, scaly horned alien."

"They're not purple or scaly—although they do have horns. Women think they're sexy."

"The horns or the aliens?"

"I was referring to their horns, but both, actually."

"Well, not me." I shuddered. Dating out of my species did not interest me.

"You don't understand what a great opportunity this is. The producers managed to get a slot for you. Do you have any idea how hard that is?" Chantelle said. "Since they've opened up the Terra-Dakon Exchange Program to all women instead of just convicted felons, women have rushed to enroll. There's a waiting list a parsec long."

"Then give someone else my slot. Slim as chances are for finding a husband, I'll hold out for a human." With more females than males on Terra, men had gotten picky, and few committed to monogamous long-term relationships anymore.

"I did some negotiating with Apogee on your behalf. I got them to sweeten the deal. You'll get a bonus." She grinned, a cat with a mouthful of bird feathers.

She could spin this as doing me a favor, but the truth was Chantelle had put the screws to Apogee because she received 10 percent of everything I earned. Besides, it was an agent's *job* to negotiate for her client. But it was all moot. "No amount of money is worth marrying an alien," I said.

"Technically, it's not a marriage; it's not a legal union on Terra." She paused dramatically. "Apogee will pay you a two-million-dollar bonus on top of your regular salary."

"Two million?" My jaw dropped. I received fifty K per episode, eight episodes per season. Sure, I earned more than the barista at the corner coffee shop, but a single "episode" took four to six weeks to shoot, and then you had to subtract Chantelle's percentage and taxes. Plus, I wasn't just supporting myself. With Devon so ill, Stormy couldn't work, so I picked up the tab for their expenses and his medical bills. We were getting by, but two million could cushion our lives. I might even get a full night's sleep without worrying what new disaster the morning would bring.

"One half up front, and the remainder after you return to Earth."

"Oh, so I get to come back?" I said drily.

Chantelle missed the sarcasm. "Of course. No one expects you to hook up with an alien for life. After a year—"

"A year?"

"The time will go fast."

"For you," I snapped.

"After a year, you'll come home, and I'll renegotiate your contract with Apogee Productions. The ratings will have gone supernova, you'll be a big star, and I'll get you a more lucrative contract." My agent's eyes lit up with dollar signs.

My career *might* pan out the way Chantelle envisioned, but I wasn't interested. The last time I'd gotten a free lunch, I was in the second grade, and some kid gave me the bologna sandwich he didn't want. I would pay for any salary increase by having to perform more outlandish stunts, and I shuddered to contemplate what could be worse than hooking up with an extraterrestrial. When my contract expired, this trained monkey planned to run away from the circus. I'd had enough "excellent adventures" to last me a lifetime. I was outta here. *Sayonara. Adios amigos.*

But two million dollars...

"So, I get a big bonus and potentially a lot more money in the long run. What's in it for the alien?" Why would he seek a creature from another planet? It had to be just as weird for him.

"A future. Dakon is critically short of women. After an asteroid strike threw the planet into an ice age—"

"The planet is in ice age?" Laughter, and not the funny kind, bubbled up and exited in a snort. Could the situation get any more ridiculous?

"Dakon is starting to recover. They get a good couple of months of sun, now. Anyway, a virus on the asteroid infected and killed most of the women and altered their DNA. Very few females are born anymore."

"So the alien would expect me to bear his

children?" I could not believe this conversation.

"He might, but you're not responsible for his expectations."

"Oh, good." I rolled my eyes. "Because I'd hate to think you had offered me two million dollars to have sex with an alien."

"You wouldn't be required to engage in sexual relations because while prostitution is no longer illegal, it is against the law to force someone into it. Apogee abides by the law, and *Sunny Weathers' Excellent Adventures* isn't a sex show."

Not yet, anyway. I gotta get out of this contract. "Why would he agree to this? He won't be getting the mate he wants."

"He won't realize it until after the show." She shrugged. "He can try again if he wants to."

The proposition sounded like a scam. We'd be deceiving, cheating the alien. And that's if it worked. He might not be human, but that didn't mean he was stupid. "He's going to notice the camera crew."

"There won't be one. They'll send a robotic microcam prototype; the Dakonians won't notice it's there. This will be the beta test. If the cambot performs to spec, they'll produce more for other shows."

"How little are they?"

Chantelle formed a circle with her thumb and index finger.

"That's still pretty big. They'll be noticed."

"You think so?" She jerked her head to a corner of her office.

Son of a production company executive! A winged orb slightly smaller than a Ping-Pong ball hovered close to the ceiling. Its body was a matte, mottled gray. Even searching for it, I'd had a hard time spotting it. I glowered at Chantelle. "I'm being videoed?"

"Prelim for the season." She nodded. "Your reluctance will be a great episode."

Sometimes I wondered whose interests she represented, mine or Apogee's. Actually, the answer was neither. Chantelle served Chantelle. Well, Sunny was going to look out for Sunny. I crossed my arms. "I'll tell the alien he's being videoed and is on a show."

"You'll void the contract, you won't receive the bonus, and you'll be stuck on Dakon until the scheduled ship picks you up."

I spoke directly to the cambot. "I won't do it. I won't sacrifice a year of my life—and it's not fair to the alien."

"I understand your reluctance—"

"Do you?" I doubted it.

My agent's attitude indicated she considered this a good opportunity, but she wasn't leaving her sister and nephew, freezing her ass off on an alien wasteland, and dating a horned extraterrestrial. "My answer is no."

Chantelle peered down her surgically perfected nose. For as much plastic surgery as she'd had, you'd have thought she worked in front of the camera. "If you refuse, Apogee will sue for breach of contract."

"Let them. I don't have any money." I acted tough; I hoped Apogee bought my bluff. They might make an example out of me, bankrupt me to deter other cast members who might be considering weaseling out of their contracts. What would happen to Devon? How would we pay for his medical care? If we were flat broke, we might be able to get him on public assistance, but that wouldn't provide the specialized level of care he needed.

Would Apogee really sue? Was one insignificant cast member like me worth it? I resented how I'd allowed them to coerce me into doing things I didn't want to do. I'd rolled over so many times, I was dizzy. The time had come to draw the line. *Show no fear.* I lifted my chin. "I won't do it."

"You'll be blacklisted from every reality show and program for life. You'll never work in this town again.

Think about it before you decide. Call me in the morning."

I got to my feet. "The answer is no. The answer will always be no."

* * * *

"Auntie Sunny!" A pint-sized powerhouse slammed into me.

I staggered backward dramatically. "Whoa, handsome! You almost knocked me over." That he'd launched himself at me meant he must be feeling better today.

"I'm not handsome, I'm a cyborg!" He was smaller than other six-year-olds, and dark smudges ringed his brown eyes, giving him the look of a wise old man in a child's body. Perhaps he was—if wisdom came with experience. He'd been through a lot.

"Cyborgs can't be handsome?"

"No! We're rough and tough and strong!" He huffed, and my heart sank as I realized he was out of breath from the race across the tiny room.

"Too tough to give your auntie a hug?" I picked him up. Had he lost weight? Skinny arms wrapped around my neck. He felt like a little bird. My heart seized. The drug treatments had to be doing some good, didn't they?

309

Stormy entered the tiny living room from the back bedroom she shared with Devon. "How did the meeting with Chantelle go?"

I gave Devon a big smooch and set him on his feet. "You won't believe what they want me to do this time." All of a sudden, the back of my neck itched with a bad feeling. Apogee wouldn't…would they? I surveyed our living room. There it was. A tiny winged orb. The cambot had followed me home! Fury ignited, and I grabbed a pillow from the sofa and batted at the camera. "Get out! Get out now!"

The camera zipped out of reach.

"Ugh! Is that an insect?" Stormy asked.

"I wish! Open the door—quick!" Swinging the pillow, I batted the camera into the hallway then slammed the door.

I scanned the ceiling. It looked clear. Hopefully, there was just the one. "That was a camera."

"That tiny thing? It looked like a fat little dragonfly." She canted her head. "Are you filming?"

I leaned against the door, battening down the hatch. "Not if I can help it."

"What do they want you to do? Snorkel in shark-infested waters? Camp in a Quonset hut in the Arctic? Rocket into space?" She was getting warmer.

"They want me to marry an alien. I told them no."

"You mean someone from another country?"

I snorted. "Uh, no. Someone from another *planet*."

Devon looked serious. "Don't do it, Auntie. Aliens have lizard tails, green faces, and red, scary eyes." Even a six-year-old recognized a bad idea when he heard one.

"No worries, handsome. I told them no." I directed my voice to the ceiling in case a cambot had sneaked in then said to Stormy, "You've heard of the Terra-Dakon Exchange Program?"

"They want you to sign up?"

"They already signed me up. Apparently, there's an alien waiting to meet me."

"A lot of women want to do it."

"Would you?"

"I might if not for Devon's medical needs, but—"

My jaw dropped. "You'd really consider it?"

"The chances of meeting a marriage-minded man here are slim. I heard Dakonians are family-oriented. She glanced at Devon. "And totally R-I-P-P-E-D," she spelled. "Like bodybuilders without the steroids."

"Where'd you hear that?"

"A commercial for the exchange program."

"Ah! It must be true if it was in an advertisement."

"I don't believe everything I hear, but it's worth looking into. It's something positive, hopeful." The light in her eyes dimmed, and her shoulders slumped.

Our parents had named their firstborn child Stormy and the second daughter Sunny, but they'd reversed the names with the personalities. By nature, my sister was optimistic, cheerful, and levelheaded. I was the tempestuous, volatile one. To see her appear so defeated meant she had bad news.

"Hey, handsome, why don't you draw me a picture of an alien?" I suggested to Devon.

"Sure, Auntie!" He raced toward the bedroom where he had a small desk. The door slammed.

"What's wrong?"

Stormy's eyes welled with tears. "Devon's doctor called. The transplant fell through. It wasn't a match. She said she doubts he'll ever find a match."

How in this day and age was this possible? We could rocket across the damn galaxy to an alien planet, but we couldn't cure a little boy with a congenital heart condition. The unfairness, my own helplessness, swelled, and I wanted to hit something. I'd been premature in ejecting the cambot. If it had been here, I could have stomped it flat.

I couldn't let Stormy see how upset I was. "We can't give up hope."

"It took two years to find this one," she said.

Donor hearts for children like Devon didn't become available often. Before he could get a replacement, someone else's child had to die, and Devon had a rare blood type, making him a difficult match for any hearts that did become available.

"But the drug treatments…"

"They're not working, and they're destroying his kidneys. By the time he gets a heart, *if* he gets one, he might need a kidney transplant."

"There has to be something that can be done." I couldn't bear to consider any other alternative.

She sniffed. "His doctor thinks he'd be a good candidate for a mechanical heart. He could be a cyborg after all." Her snort of laughter ended in tears.

"Well, that's good news! Isn't it?"

"Insurance won't cover it. Surgery and recovery would cost over a million and a half dollars—more with rehab."

No deliberation was necessary. I did a 180. "Devon will get a mechanical heart!" I flung open the door.

The cambot zipped inside and flew a donut around

my head. I stared into a red light glowing like a tiny eye, indicating filming was active. "You've got yourself a bride. But I want the entire bonus up front." I'd contact Chantelle and let her earn her commission by working out the details.

Stormy stared. "What-what are you doing?"

"I didn't get a chance to tell you. To sweeten the deal, to get me to agree to hook up with an alien, Apogee offered a two-million-dollar bonus. That should pay for Devon's heart."

My sister shook her head. "Oh no. You can't—I can't let you sacrifice—" But her face lightened with hope.

"For Devon, it's no sacrifice."

"I'm all done, Auntie!" Devon scooted out of the bedroom, waving a paper. He ran to me, a little boy with a bright smile who deserved a bright future. He was my sister's child, but we'd raised him together, and if anything happened to him, I wouldn't be able to stand it.

I blinked away tears. "Bring it here. Let's see!"

He'd drawn a green man with a lizard's tail and short T. rex arms. He had a single eye like a cyclops, and curving out of his head were ram-like horns. "Very nice." I smiled at him.

I crossed my fingers, hoping my alien didn't resemble the one in Devon's drawing.

Chapter Two

Darq

"Okay, men, listen up." Enoki, our council leader, raised his arms, and waited until the rumble of voices quieted. "One hundred women will arrive, twice as many as the first time."

"*Obah! Obah!*" We cheered and slapped each other's backs. Though many ships had landed with supplies, this was the first in two years to bring what we really desired: females.

After the commotion died down, Enoki glanced at Andrea, a Terran female mated to a healer named Groman.

"One week from today," Andrea announced. She assisted our leader in his dealings with Earth. My brother's mate, Starr, had said Andrea was a *hacker*, supposedly a bad thing on their planet, but her abilities had helped us tremendously in using the equipment the Terrans had installed.

"Obah!" I cheered with the others. My mate was arriving! Deep in my bones, I sensed her presence already. The winds of fate had decreed I would get a mate in this shipment.

"As with the first time, each tribe was allotted a specific number of females based on clan population." Standing on a riser, Enoki motioned to baskets lined up behind him. "Your names were whittled on a chit and placed in these baskets. From each one, Andrea will draw an appropriate number of chits. Those men will exchange the name chit for a numbered one, which will determine the order in which you pick your mate. Any questions?"

"If we're not chosen, how long before the next shipment?" someone asked.

Enoki looked at Andrea.

"I don't think the next time will take as long," she said. "They've worked out the details now." Once it had become public Earth's government was using the treaty to get rid of its female criminals, the exchange program had been put on hold.

"But how long?"

"I don't know, but I'll try to find out," she replied.

"Let's focus on the positive today," Enoki said. "We have names to draw. Andrea?"

Her braided hair swung like ropes as she stepped onto the riser. Her skin was a rich brown tone, slightly darker than our own. Though shorter than a Dakonian, she was among the tallest of the Terran women. Many considered her comely, myself included. I hoped my mate looked like her.

Her teeth gleamed white in a crescent grin. Chits rattled as she shook the basket. "Is everybody ready?"

I was bursting with ready.

Until the Terrans, in search of the illuvian ore they needed to light their cities and power their spaceships, "discovered" Dakon, I had become resigned to never knowing a mate's love. Then we'd learned our two species were biologically compatible, and when Terra had offered to send us priceless females in exchange for worthless rock, well, everything changed.

My brother, Torg, had acquired a female in the first group. Watching him and Starr Conner so much in love, and now expecting a child, made me ache all the more for what they had.

I often caught them meshing lips. *Kissing,* Starr called it. Both seemed to enjoy it very much, and although I'd found the idea of pressing mouths revolting at first, I'd gotten accustomed to seeing it and had begun to wonder what it felt like. After my mate arrived, I would find out.

Enoki peered into a ledger. "The first tribe is

Viltor's. They have five chits allotted." He signaled to Andrea.

She reached deep inside the basket and fished around before pulling out a wooden chip and handing it to Enoki.

"Baranko," he called.

"Obah!" Baranko grinned from ear to ear. His tribemates pounded him on the back in congratulations, but I saw jealousy on the faces of others. I swallowed my own envy. *My time will come. This is just the beginning.* The winning of a female in Viltor's tribe in no way lessened the odds for Torg's clan.

Andrea drew another name.

"Roqa," our leader announced.

After the last man's name was drawn from Viltor's tribe, the five winners congregated at the back of the meeting place while the unchosen stomped away in angry disappointment. A blast of cold air swept into the room as they shoved the flaps aside and exited. There would be more losers than winners, more unhappy people than happy ones today.

Dakon had fifteen tribes, and I had to wait while twelve of them went through the process before thcy got to Torg's tribe. By then, the crowd had thinned.

Enoki ran his finger down the ledger. "Torg's tribe gets three chits."

This was it! I stood up straighter. I felt sorry for my fellow tribemates who would lose, but excitement swelled to a crescendo inside me. The winds had predicted my fortune. Would Andrea give me a nod before she gave the chit to Enoki? Our acquaintance was by sight, but she and Starr were close friends. Basket mouths were wide, and Andrea could see the chit before she handed it to Enoki.

That would be cheating.

She pulled out a name.

"Sural," Enoki called.

My tribemate bounded forward, and I congratulated him heartily.

Two more. One of those was mine.

Andrea dipped into the basket.

"Korbett." Enoki nodded at my tribemate standing next to me.

He grabbed me in a kel hug, and I thumped him on the back. "Congratulations," I said.

"Final one," Enoki announced.

This was it! I shifted on the balls of my feet, prepared to leap forward and claim my right.

Andrea dipped into the basket.

Alien Mate

* * *

Alien Attraction story blurb

How insane is it to marry an alien as a publicity stunt?

I'm Sunny Weathers. You probably recognize me from my TV show, Sunny Weathers' Excellent Adventures. I've had to perform a lot of crazy stunts in my career, but this one takes the cake! The producers are sending me to another planet to become an alien's mail order bride. I'm not allowed to tell anybody it's a gimmick, and as soon my contract is up, I'll be leaving planet Dakon. Unfortunately, I hadn't counted on my attraction to Mr. Tall, "Darq," and Handsome...

I'm Darq. The moment I laid eyes on the female with pretty mud-colored hair and a sunny smile, I knew she was mine. Competition for females is fierce, and I was determined to claim a mate from the latest shipment from Earth, so I broke the rules. If anyone finds out, my own brother would banish me to the icy wilderness, and I'd lose my mate. I will do anything to keep her...

* * * *

Read the rest of Sunny and Darq's story in **Alien Attraction (Alien Mate 2)**

Subscribe to my reader newsletter to get a free alien romance. **KRASH*: Dakonian Alien Mail Order Brides : https://carabristol.com/newsletter/*

Other Titles by Cara Bristol

Get a complete printable book list at

https://carabristol.com/printable-booklist/

Alien Mate series

Alien Mate (Book 1)
Alien Attraction (Book 2)
Alien Intention (Book 3)
Alien Mischief (Book 4)
Alien Mate Complete Series Boxed Set

Dakonian Alien Mail-Order Brides (An Alien Mate spinoff series)

Darak
Aton
Caid
Sixx
Kord
Braxx
Krash
Dakonian Alien Mail Order Brides Boxed Set Vol 1
Dakonian Alien Mail Order Brides Boxed Set Vol. 2

Forbidden Bonds

Alien With Benefits
Alien Incognito
Alien Undone
Alien Disgraced
Alien in Disguise

Alien Castaways

Alien Mate

Chameleon
Wingman
Psy
Shadow
Inferno
Tigre
Alien Castaway Vol. 1 (Books 1-3)
Alien Castaways Vol 2 (Books 4-6)
Alien Castaways Complete Series (Books 1-6)

Genmate Dilemma trilogy (An Alien Castaways Spinoff Serial)

Genmate Mistaken
Genmate Forsaken
Genmate Imperiled
Genmate Dilemma Complete Series boxed set

Cyborg Force

Blown Away
Gale Force
Vortex
Maelstrom
Cyborg Force Collection One (Books 1-2)
Cyborg Force Collection Two (Books 3-4)

Men of Mettle cyborg romance series

Cyborg Protector (Book1)
Cyborg Husband (Book 1.5)
Cyborg Rogue (Book 2)
Cyborg Boss (Book 3)
Cyborg Heat (Book 4)
Cyborg Mate (Book 5)
Cyborg Rescuer (Book 6)

Cyborg Commander (Book 7)
Men of Mettle Cyborg Romance Collection

Breeder sci-fi romance series

Breeder (Book 1)
Terran (Book 2)
Warrior (Book 3)
Breeder Boxed Set

Alien Dragon Shifters

Under Fyre
Line of Fyre
Playing with Fyre
Kiss of Fyre: Alien Dragon Shifters Boxed Set

Nonfiction

Naughty Words for Nice Writers A Romance Novel
Thesaurus
You're not Ugly to Look At: Conversations with my
Husband

.

About Cara Bristol

USA Today bestselling author Cara Bristol writes science fiction romance about tough alien and cyborg heroes who fall hard for gutsy heroines.

Cara is a homebody who married a wanderer. When she's not writing or being distracted by squirrels cavorting outside her office window, she enjoys reading and traveling the world with her husband. Topping her bucket list is visiting all seven continents and petting a squirrel.

Cara's Website
https://carabristol.com/

Reader Newsletter
https://carabristol.com/newsletter/

Facebook
https://www.facebook.com/cara.bristol.3

Bristol's Book Babes (Reader Facebook group)
https://www.facebook.com/groups/1761424733891183/

BookBub profile
https://www.bookbub.com/profile/cara-bristol

Instagram (@authorcarabristol)
https://www.instagram.com/authorcarabristol/